INTO
THE
SHADOWLAND

THE SECRET OF
THE LAST
NEANDERTHALS

By
J.M.G. SCHMIDT

Publisher: Books to Hook Publishing, LLC.

ISBN: 979-8-89283-297-7

Our ancestors lie dormant within us,
clever beings and gifted hunters.

1

It all began with an unusual wildlife accident.

Forty-three miles east of Salt Lake City, Highway UT-150 twists through the heart of Uinta–Wasatch–Cache National Park. Lilly Feron focused on steering her Jeep along the tight roadway, densely lined with tall, dark pines. Switchbacks and long mountainside climbs forced her to slow down again and again. She drove wildly, as if something was driving her, urging her to hurry. As the road unwound and stretched over a high meadow, she continued to follow this inner voice.

When tall trees began to surround the highway once again, however, the stillness transformed into a chaotic scene: flashing police lights, a towing service, and some curious onlookers blocked the thoroughfare. Lilly slammed the brakes. The seat belts tightened, sending her passenger's horn-rimmed glasses flying.

"Sorry, Fred!"

Flicking her hazard lights on, she maneuvered the Jeep onto the hard shoulder and crawled cautiously toward a uniformed guard beckoning them closer. *That must be the ranger who called me*, she thought. He'd suspected that a common gray wolf was the body struck by the car, but couldn't be sure of it. A few feet away, she saw a demolished Toyota Prius on the embankment. Fred was still fumbling for his glasses when Lilly got out.

"Ms. Feron? .... Thank you for coming so early. We need your expertise. I'm Stan Hardy, Utah Department of Conservation, and I've been a ranger in the area for a month. Just call me Stan."

With a friendly grin, the tall, lanky ranger grabbed his wide-brimmed hat, showed his badge and sheepishly pushed his undersized shirt into his pants. He reminded Lilly of Stan Laurel, the English comedian—his features almost a caricature of the man. The coincidence of his surname being shared with Laurel's famous sidekick made the resemblance all the more uncanny. Still, she tried to look past his outward appearance as he began gesticulating in the direction of the wreck.

Stan Hardy certainly wanted to appear professional. Visibly anxious to get everything right, he noted the time: 8:23 a.m. He cleared his throat and pointed to the Prius. "A wildlife accident. As I'm sure you'd expect, ma'am. The driver was injured pretty badly and is on the way to the emergency room. Must have been a terrible fright to lose control of the car like that—no wonder when a predatory animal comes running in front of you after that godawful bend."

Lilly sighed softly. In a moment, he would ask if the animal came from her wolf park. "I'm sorry for the driver, Stan...." She looked around searchingly. "And for the wolf, too. I take it he didn't survive?"

"That's right, come over!" The ranger trudged over the scree toward two knee-high boulders. "Poor thing must have been thrown into the air. Looks kind of strange, doesn't it?" He gave her a questioning look and rubbed his long chin. "I have to ask... is he from your park?"

Feron Wolf Park is a familiar name to researchers around the world. Lilly's father, biologist Leo Feron, started building the facility with a small team in the 1990s. In the high country of Utah, he hand-reared dozens of wolves and researched their behavior, earning him the title of the wolf whisperer. Lilly grew up at the park; studying biology and veterinary medicine was the natural next step. After her father died suddenly in 2020, she took over the management of Feron Wolf Park at the age of just twenty-six.

Dutifully, Stan asked again: "Your fences, Ms. Feron... I strongly advise you to check them. If the animal came from your enclosure ...."

"Our fences are tight, Stan, they're secure. Don't worry about that! Feel free to pay us a surprise visit and check. We adhere to the official guidelines.... I'm sure you are familiar with them?"

Hardy lifted his hat, grinned sheepishly and scratched his forehead. He didn't seem to have a clue about the details, so Lilly rattled off a handful of reminders:

"Thirteen-foot-high, heavy-duty steel fences with forty-five-degree angles, thirty-nine-inch-wide guard rails, security locks, surveillance cameras and so on. The full gamut, you know? This is Fred, my intern, by the way."

The men exchanged handshakes and wary introductions. Fred, over-weight, red-haired and with a rosy complexion, stood like a comedic contrast to the tanned, skinny ranger. But the two were not only differ-ent in appearance. While Stan, odd-looking as he was, generally coped well with challenges, Fred was one of those people who seemed to carry an inbuilt magnet for disaster. Mishaps and blunders accompanied him throughout his life, yet Lilly did not give up on him. She felt he held a certain potential, even if it hadn't yet made itself known.

"Freddy is doomed to check the enclosures at regular intervals. It's part of your training, isn't it?" Lilly patted him on the shoulder. "Tell Stan about your *favorite* job!"

Fred rolled his eyes and blushed. "She's right, Mr. Hardy. To be honest, the route around the fences is frickin' long, and I have to walk it while checkin' for weak spots, whatever the weather. It's my weekly training session, so to speak. My boss probably wants me to lose weight so I can fit through the bars."

Everyone laughed. With the tension eased, Fred continued on, describing in great detail the four enclosures that housed their wolves.

He was delighted not to have ended up in a farm zoo; he had nothing against that, but he wanted to become an animal keeper with genuine knowledge. Above all else, he explained, he was captivated by the social behavior of packs, and Feron provided a 'pretty much perfect' place for him to explore it.

Stan listened attentively and promised to visit very soon. In the meantime, Lilly had turned to the dead wolf, examining him from all sides, bending over him until her smooth blond hair almost graced his dirty fur. With wide-open, glassy eyes, he lay in a dark red pool, his long tongue hanging from his mouth as if making a final, desperate attempt to reclaim his own blood.

At first glance, Lilly was surprised by the animal's physical appearance. Compared to the enclosure wolves she knew inside out, this one had died in a pitiful, emaciated state.

"Please make a note, Stan," she declared in a matter-of-fact tone, "that this wolf is not from our facility. Hell, he's not even from this region. Just take a look at him! He's been on a long journey."

"Seems like he could use the rest," Stan remarked dryly. "No, no, it's awful sad, but I'll still be glad if your enclosures remain sealed. I think we can put this whole matter behind us quickly." He pulled a small brush from his inside pocket and by habit ran it gently over his uniform. "The police and the insurance company will take it from here."

For the freshly appointed Ranger, this answered the most important question: the wolf park posed no danger. He returned the clothes brush to his pocket and, turning to the accident scene, asking a group of curious onlookers to move on.

Fred, who was in a great mood, sucked in his stomach, made funny faces and took selfies in front of the flashing vehicles. Pulling on a set of bright yellow rubber gloves, Lilly began to examine the animal's lifeless body. Her hand felt something unusual under the fur: a hard, immovable object lodged deep in the wolf's neck. This injury, which appeared a few weeks old, was unlikely to have stemmed from the collision with the Prius. For now, the vet kept her suspicions to herself.

"If you don't mind, Ranger, we'll take him to the clinic for further examinations," she called to Stan.

"Very well, I mean, that's fine. Thank you, Ms. Feron." Stan was relieved that disposing of the carcass wouldn't fall on his shoulders. He cleared his throat and asked the final question on his list. "It seems to me that this one's physique is different from the local wolves. It doesn't exactly look like an ordinary..."

"Indeed, this is not a typical gray wolf." Lilly cut him off. She wrapped a tape measure around one of the wolf's hind legs, stretched and measured the tail and opened the mouth. "The body proportions, the skull, its teeth... It's all very strange!"

"No problem," Stan quickly rebutted. "Unnecessary details only complicate matters. Just let me know when you've found out more about his origins. That would be very kind of you, Ms. Feron."

He sat on one of the boulders to fill out a document on his cell phone. It appeared to him that if the wolf had wandered into the area, then the situation would be all the better for it. That wouldn't get the opponents of local wolves up in arms, for a change.

"He's dead anyway, one less thing to worry about," he muttered to himself as he continued typing.

"Excuse me?" The words had hit a nerve with Lilly. She knew the arguments of wolf opponents only too well and, for what felt like the thousandth time in her life, decided to set something straight. She stood up in front of the ranger. "As I'm sure you know, *Stan*, not a single person was killed by wolves last year, not a single one... worldwide! So, if you ask me, they're not exactly a major threat. The year before, there was exactly one, and he had rabies. The real problem is us, Stan, not the wolves."

Startled, the cell phone slipped from Stan's hand and clattered onto the dusty roadside. "It's all right," he reassured her as he bent down to pick it up. "I'm sure you're right; I agree with you. And there are dogs guarding livestock and electric fences around the pastures. It's probably just that age-old fear in us humans. Something instinctive, y'know."

"Exactly, the fear from fairy tales and myths!"

Lilly understood that Stan's role as a ranger meant walking a line between protecting the wilderness and serving commercial interests. This made it all the more important to open the rookie's eyes. She was uncompromising in her commitment to preservation. She knew only too well what was at stake.

"Above all, you're working for nature, Stan, and nature needs genetic diversification. Are you familiar with the WWF's *Living Planet Report 2022*? Maybe you're not... not enough people are. But, in any case, it states that wild animal populations have declined by an average of seventy percent over the past fifty years. Seventy percent!"

"Ouch!"

"Yes, *ouch*! And it's humans alone that are responsible for this. We can't survive without a single species and certainly not without large, wild predators, which—I'm sure you're aware—include wolves. They aren't merely a *nuisance*. They are eco-engineers who help to make resources available and create ecological niches for countless other creatures. They lay the foundation for many insect species, for a start, which in turn fuel birds, bats and, heck, the entire food chain. So, yeah, they are damn important."

Stan slumped slightly but continued to listen attentively.

"Listen, Stan, I don't want to discourage you —on the contrary! There is reason for hope. We know what's going on and we're trying to turn things around. The keyword is *rewilding*. We are restoring landscapes to what they once were. Biotopes are being restored, the drainage of wetlands is being stopped... we're even bringing large mammals back into the ecosystems. This is how natural processes are getting back on track. It works, too. Before long, a diverse biodiversity emerges."

Satisfied with his selfie shoot, Fred sat down next to Stan, who seemed somehow to have shrunk while squatted on the stone. They watched as Lilly trudged to the Wrangler, opened the trunk, and dug out a fleece blanket.

A pick-up truck rolled up behind her at the side of the road. With the windows halfway down, the driver, smoking a cigarette, gazed at the dead wolf. From the backseat, a sheepdog barked loudly into the forest.

"Look, he's barking at the pine trees!" mocked Fred.

"How strange," Stan said.

"Maybe a coyote is hiding in the thicket. They can smell a carcass a mile off." Lilly threw the blanket to Fred. "Could you wrap up the wolf, please!"

"Wolves are not welcome here," the driver sneered from the pick-up, dropping his cigarette butt onto the tarmac.

Stan stood up and walked toward the truck. "You shouldn't stop here," he warned firmly. "Please keep driving, sir, and don't throw any more cigarettes out the window!"

The man drove off with a grim set to his jaw, his sheepdog still barking at the thicket.

Lilly thanked Stan. "You see, *that's* what I mean. You can't get anywhere with them. They have no idea how useful wolves are."

Stan brushed the dust from his pants, content that he'd redeemed his earlier clumsy impression. "Where the wolf hunts, the forest grows," he said, uncertainly. "It's a Russian proverb. My grandfather used to say it from time to time on our walks."

"How true! Above all, be the guardian of the forest!" Lilly encouraged as charmingly as she could. "It's much easier to preserve an intact ecosystem than to restore a destroyed one. I'd love to take you on a tour of the real wilderness."

"That would be great, Ms. Feron!"

Lilly was glad that he understood her appeals. She looked at her watch. A quick post-mortem was needed.

Stan helped to load the wolf, said goodbye politely and waved behind them.

2

The morning is fresh. The air is clear. The accident site has been cleared and swept, and the last vehicle has departed the scene. A peaceful silence once again reigns over highway UT-150. The spicy scent of wood, resin, and summer mushrooms wafts over the earth, and the soft melodies of buzzing insects and chirping birds have returned.

Out of nowhere, another inhabitant of the forest emerges. Gigantic, as strong as a tree and as silent as a wildcat, it slinks through the branches, pauses, listens, and continues to wind its stocky, powerful, humanlike body toward the road. Stopping to listen once again, the creature sniffs eagerly at the blood on the roadside.

The noise of the high-headed people, whom his people call bobos, has died off. They, who resemble him but seem so fragile, were here, took it and are now gone.

He must get it back, and he will. After all, he is Omu: the animals of the forest give him information, and the voices of the mountains, the moon, and the stars show him the way. He has been hunting the wolf for a long time; he must not lose him now.

He had been watching from the cover of the undergrowth for quite a while. Among the many lights and other bobos, he saw a large redhead and a woman with hair like the sun. A small wolf, which they called a dog, had barked in his direction, but Omu hid from their gaze.

As the bobos finally departed, he realized that they were taking the wolf with them, dragging away the very prize he had been stalking for days.

They are too fast, he thought. The wolf disappeared with them; the relic disappeared with the wolf and, with it, the secret symbol that he must retrieve—the symbol no one must see because that would betray Omu and his entire clan… forever.

A low, disappointed growl emerges from the depths of his strong lungs. Exhausted, he settles down in the soft leaves, lowers his mighty skull and rests his bulging forehead on the knees of his short, stocky legs.

Is this the end? Was it all in vain?

3

Lilly parked at the delivery entrance, close beside the wolf enclosures. This area housed refrigerated meat, various storage rooms, and a small holding room for the temporary storage of animal carcasses. The residential section, which encompassed Lilly's beloved veterinary clinic, was located on the far side of the building, connected by a maze of corridors.

As usual, the park's wolf packs were eagerly awaiting their return, having sensed the low hum of the approaching car minutes before it arrived. Lilly had long been convinced that many animals have a seventh sense, an unexplained instinct that allows them to rapidly anticipate dangers—or opportunities—and respond as such.

She vividly remembered a PBS documentary in which thought transmission between humans and dogs was apparent. In the experiment, two independent cameras were synchronized: one with Jaydee, the dog, and the other with Mrs. Smart, his owner. Mrs. Smart had been told to stay in the city until she was instructed to return home to Jaydee. She took a cab to make sure Jaydee couldn't hear the familiar engine noise of her car.

The experiment was repeated several times, and without fail the dog—who had spent most of the day dozing—ran to the window shortly after Mrs. Smart set off for home. To Lilly, this mental connection confirmed what she already knew; dogs, and her wolves therefore, truly can sense their owner's homecoming, even from a distance away.

Disputes are commonplace in captive wolf packs. It was usual for rivalries to flare up in the enclosure when Lilly arrived. The hierarchy was repeatedly put to the test. But today, something was different. There was something else in the air: the scent of a foreign rival.

When Lilly opened the trunk, the scent wafted through the steel fence and toward the nearest wolf enclosure, where the pack homed in on the supposed intruder. The animals raised their hackles and darted their ears forward. With their tails outstretched and every muscle tensed up, they followed every movement around the vehicle.

"Calm down!" Lilly called over. "I know you've scented him. But this one is none of your business."

While Lilly unlocked the steel gate, Fred removed the dead wolf from the fleece blanket and carried him through the corridors to the clinic.

Although pleased with his responsibility, he knew that this was the realm of his boss. Lilly Feron called it the *head office*, the venue that hosted most of her days and nights. This head office blurred clinic, office, and living space: a couch, desk, and green cabinets flowed into an operating table and instrument rack, separated only by a screen. A stainless-steel crate gleamed in the corner.

Behind a pass-through was the cozy dining area and kitchen that claimed most of Fred's spare time. The kitchen's panoramic window looked over the extensive courtyard and surrounding woodland, interrupted only by the gravel where mail deliverers, tradespeople, and visitors parked.

As Fred entered the clinic, he recalled the lesson his boss had delivered on his first day as a trainee:

"As a veterinarian, I am a general practitioner, psychologist, surgeon, dentist, and obstetrician. In my private life, I am the head of the family... and a wolfess."

With the stiff predator in his arms, Fred sweated and struggled not to stumble. "He's not half as big as I am," he groaned, "but he's as heavy as lead, believe me."

"You can do it, Fred. Just get him onto the scales!"

Panting, Fred stood on the scales with the wolf. "Together, three hundred forty-three pounds." He lifted the cadaver onto the bowl-shaped stainless steel table, then weighed himself. "One hundred eighty-seven… so the wolf's one fifty-six!"

Out of breath, he marveled at the lean male's surprising bulk. Lilly, watching closely, knew she'd have to investigate.

The vet measured while her trainee noted the shoulder height, head–torso length and the length of the legs, muzzle, tail, ears, and teeth. The light-colored coat was coarse, thick and short. His powerful hind legs, small ears, slightly shorter, curved tail and robust appearance, reminded Lilly of past lectures on Canis lupus, the gray wolf with a strong tribal history.

Looking over his short muzzle and immense teeth, she pondered momentarily, opened her laptop, and began comparing the dead animal to subspecies of the gray wolf. None of them, however, came close to the weighty, alien physique of the specimen laying in her home office.

Fred sipped a Coke and watched her intently through his horn-rimmed glasses. It looked to him as though the more his boss investigated, the more perplexed she grew. Still, he didn't dare say anything.

"The amazing part is," Lilly said at last, "that it doesn't seem to be an ordinary gray. It almost looks like …." She paused again. "That's incredible!"

"What's incredible, boss?" asked Fred, his tension fusing with a new-found curiosity.

"Well, look here… I mean… he looks one hundred percent like…"

She tapped on a picture that depicted the black-and-white outline of a wolf. Next to it stood the silhouette of a man, a little over one hundred seventy-five centimeters tall. Compared to him, the predator looked remarkably beefy and robust.

"... this. That's the one, Freddy. It's got to be. But... the thing is, we've thought it to be extinct... for a few thousand years." She turned suddenly to face him, as if saying it aloud had made the absurdity of the discovery dawn upon her.

"A friggin' long time ago, I'd say!"

"Absolutely! If it is, *if* it is a Beringian Wolf, it would be a real sensation, comparable to the rediscovery of the coelacanth in '87, the living fossil from the age of dinosaurs. The Beringian wolves belong to a population that lived during the Ice Age in what is now Alaska, the Yukon and northern British Columbia. It goes without saying that herbivores were much larger back then, and a hell of a lot stronger than any living today."

"Beringian wolf, did you say?"

"Yes, look!" She turned the screen toward Fred. "See, compared to a gray wolf, it is much more robust." She traced her finger along the image. "You can see how it has a far stronger jaw, a wider palate and larger fangs about the size of its skull."

"Looks fierce."

"Well, you wouldn't mess with it. They could bite with the same force as a hyena today, and it could take on the megafauna of the Pleistocene—think wild horses, steppe bison, caribou, forest musk oxen and even mammoths." The trainee nodded. "But what makes him *so* heavy, Freddie, are his bones, his skull, and his teeth."

"I see. Oh yeah, now I remember!" Fred blurted, "I saw something about it on Reddit."

"What did you read about, Fred?"

"The Beringian wolf! A couple of weeks ago, some guy from Montana claimed to have spotted one near Salmon River. None of the chat participants believed him."

"And rightly so! I wouldn't have believed it either."

"Conceivable now, though, isn't it? He probably saw this guy here!"

They both looked over their shoulder at the cadaver.

"As unbelievable as it sounds, it really could be," Lilly replied, taken aback. "The wolf must have covered over three hundred and seventy miles."

"Is that possible?"

"It sounds a long way for you, but not for him. When wolves become sexually mature, they often wander out of their pack's territory. They cover long distances, walking for weeks and avoiding towns and lakes… anywhere with human life."

Lilly took one of the paws in her hand. It was dirty and cold and as large as a man's fist. "Even for this powerhouse, though, that would be an unusually long jaunt…" She hesitated, stroking the animal's ribs gently. "Of course, it's possible that something else could have been driving it," she said thoughtfully.

Standing there open-mouthed, Fred resembled a schoolboy hearing his first ghost stories. And, in a way, it seemed to him that the body before them was not all that different from a ghost—the remains of something long thought to have left Earth behind.

"What might that have been?" he asked in a daze.

Lilly didn't respond and instead gave him a friendly pat on the hip.

"Time for feeding. Legs of venison are on the menu today. I'll see you in the afternoon. Maybe you can find out some more about this guy from Montana for me; that would be very helpful."

4

Now alone with the carcass, Lilly donned her gown, mask, rubber gloves, and safety goggles, stepped to the operating table, and began neatly shaving the fur surrounding the neck wound. Before long, she again felt what she had noticed at the accident site: a broken, smooth, evenly shaped wooden shaft protruding an inch from the half-healed wound. With some effort, she tried to jiggle it back and forth, but it was firmly lodged in the vertebral arch. So, she removed the surrounding skin and muscle tissue with several skilled scalpel cuts to see into the deeper layers.

In front of the entry point into the vertebra, the wooden shaft appeared to be wrapped with string or sinew. With caution, Lilly used the electric circular saw to open the bone. Blood and splinters splattered onto her mask and goggles until, at last, the foreign body became loose. She placed it on a plate, removed her rubber gloves and cleaned her goggles. Then, she inspected the object from all sides.

At the end of the shaft was a peculiar, razor-sharp tip, one and a half inches wide and twice as long. Lilly recognized it as a blade crafted from horn, ivory or bone. Minuscule barbs down each length had anchored it in the vertebra. The spinal canal had been spared; otherwise, the wounded animal would have hardly been able to survive.

She had not expected this. After slowly sliding the uncleaned blade into a plastic bag, Lilly removed her work clothes, sat on a surgical stool, and closed her eyes to think in peace.

The hunting of this wonderful animal was as tragic as it was strange. It was astonishing enough that a Beringian wolf, long thought to be extinct, had dragged itself three hundred and seventy miles south. Stranger still was the use of such an unusual hunting instrument. What kind of strange person could wield such a weapon? The thought made her flinch.

Wolf howls were piercing the forest when Lilly dialed Stan Hardy's number and told him of her findings. The ranger thanked her for the information, hopeful of disguising the fact that he was disgruntled at the idea of the situation being more complex than he had hoped.

"What sort of lunatic lurks in the mountains and kills wolves with such a strange weapon? My agency already has enough problems with the damn poaching and, believe me, we're doing everything we can to catch the bastards. And then, right when you think you're getting a handle on it, along comes some crackpot trying to experiment with his own cruel methods. On top of that, he has an injured motorist on his conscience."

Lilly avoided bothering the officer with the story about the Beringian wolf. She wanted to follow up on the lead herself before handing it over to the authorities. Nevertheless, she knew Stan should take care of the criminal side, and advised him to cooperate with the forensic lab of the Fish and Wildlife Service.

"I'll send it to you right away," she promised. "You've never seen anything like it, Stan. Give it to the lab. Have them examine it for DNA traces. With any luck, you'll be able to track down the culprit."

"You can count on it, Ms. Feron. And thank you for calling."

5

Stan Hardy was ten when he realized his appearance was bizarre. It became clear that he didn't have to crack jokes to make others laugh. It wasn't particularly funny to him, so he decided to behave as inconspicuously as possible from then on. He dressed in neutral colors, was clean and polite, said only the bare minimum, and avoided confrontation. While this carefully-practiced way of living did succeed in keeping him out of bullies' aim, it made friendship hard to come by. If his classmates went to pop concerts, he went to classical recitals or on long hikes with his grandfather. While they lingered after school in noisy packs, he slipped home alone and lost himself in his books. With quiet diligence, he navigated high school like a stowaway.

He had already adjusted to life as a single man when he met a blind violinist named Margaret Keller in the cloakroom of the BYU Music Building in South Salt Lake. The attendant was struggling to locate Margaret's coat, so Stan helped her pat down each coat until she found it. Unintentionally, their hands brushed several times. Stan didn't let on, but Margaret could hear his heart throbbing.

After she had found her coat, Stan took out his little clothes brush and brushed it over gently. It was a gesture Margaret would come to know him for, and it was one that attracted her. She asked him to accompany her home, and Stan's single life came to a surprising end.

Today, the life he longed for was within his grasp; he just needed to decide on a career. Yet the wild had long been calling to him, inspired by the grandfather he was raised by. When the role of a ranger in Uinta–Wasatch–Cache National Park became available, it was a natural fit.

A quarter of the park, a vast sweep of land some three thousand four hundred square miles in size, lay in wilderness, spared for now from the usual marks of destruction. However, most of the natural tract, which remained completely untouched just a few decades ago, has developed into one of the nation's most visited forests, offering an Eldorado for skiers, snowboarders, hikers, mountain bikers, campers, anglers, boaters, swimmers, and horse riders.

Hunting, though, was what drew more people here than anything else. Almost all of Utah's predators, from bobcats and foxes to black bears and coyotes, are hunted. Yet some still survive.

Wolves were virtually extinct until their reintroduction to the northern Rocky Mountains in 1995. Today, authorities can confirm at least a few dozen animals in the state. Predators, in particular, have a significant impact on biodiversity. Studies show that they preserve the population of their prey, not eliminate it. If the opposite were true, they would wipe themselves out. Nature needs balance.

As a ranger for the Utah Division of Wildlife Resources, Stan Hardy was caught between two fronts: The trade associations were on one side, and the conservation organizations on the other. Both had their place in society, his agency was told. Ever since the morning he met Lilly Feron, however, he had been pondering whether the institution he worked for gave nature the support it deserved. It dawned on him that she was probably right: the notion of predators as a danger to people and their livestock was misleading.

The diehards screamed the loudest, while the prioritization of economic interests gradually decimated the last intact habitats of flora and fauna. Lilly's words had left a stark impression on Stan, yet he was unsure whether he possessed the courage to speak out in favor of conservation.

Once the initial analyses had indicated that a poacher had wounded the wolf perfidiously with a primitive hunting weapon, Stan's outrage had driven him to pursue the matter further. First, he applied for a DNA analysis, which he did not expect to succeed. He also asked a trainee to scour chat forums for information on similar hunting methods. In the meantime, he called the County Jail Administration in Salt Lake City, asking for more information on an inmate he had read about in the *Salt Lake Tribune*. His name was Jack Manchin, and he was in Salt Lake County Metro Jail for repeated poaching. Hardy hoped that talking to an insider might shed some light on the case.

On short notice, he made an appointment to visit at lunchtime, ordered two hot cappuccinos, and soon sat opposite the convict in the sparsely furnished visitors' room.

"Mr. Manchin, thank you for agreeing to talk," he began the conversation in his usual polite manner and pushed a coffee mug toward the rough-looking man. The ranger feared his tone had already sounded patronizing; after all, inmates had nothing but time.

"Keep it short!" Manchin didn't look to be in much of a mood for anything. He had had a rifle tattooed on his neck, which did little to ease Hardy's nerves. More than anything, though, the poacher looked exhausted; his cheeks and nose were red. Stan wondered whether the dilated blood vessels were due to alcoholism or frostbite. He thought it was probably both.

"I've read your file," the ranger began calmly. "Don't worry, I'm not asking about your motives. Honestly, I don't care why you went on your little hunting adventure in the national park, y'know, an area where hunting sea eagles is strictly forbidden. You'd better ask yourself why you shoot one of these rare birds of prey from its nest."

For an instant, he saw consternation in Manchin's expression, which quickly turned to arrogance before finally settling on lust. Lust that he assumed to arise from the mere thought of the hunt. Then, his face darkened again. After all, the eagle hunt had not ended well. He had made the mistake of boasting about it in the hunting chat, giving himself away.

"Do you have a question?" he hissed bitterly. "Still got work to do."

Stan got straight to the point: "Can a hunter like you kill a wolf with a javelin?"

Manchin looked puzzled, caught himself, and spent a moment wondering: "Impossible, man, forget it! Wolves are damn rare and damn smart, much smarter than a joker like you! Do you want to kill him with a spear? If you do, you'll have to get close to it first. Very close! And that's not easy, believe me."

He laughed snidely. Stan, meanwhile, eagerly took notes.

"Sure, I know about hunting. But that kind of shit is not for me. After you find his scent, the wolf's, you'll still have to wait a long time, maybe hours, even days. The best place to wait is in a tree. Right where his path is. Then, you have to do the deed from up there. You understand what I mean? You just... *Bam*, from up there in the tree. And in that instance, the spear is faster." Smacking his lips, he sipped his cappuccino, satisfied.

"From the tree," Stan repeated and wrote it down.

"But forget it! The wolf is agile. It senses danger and is gone in a flash if it hears the slightest sound. You only have one shot, understand? Just one throw. Miss it and he's gone. I can tell you that the hunter who succeeds at something like that has it in him."

Stan listened, spellbound, as his hand kept scribbling.

The poacher looked into the ranger's eyes before asking his final question. "So, tell me... has someone managed to do that?" he finished the coffee. "Tell you what, I'd like to meet him. Must be a lunatic or a genius. He's nothing in the middle. Or do you think I'm that brilliant? I'm not, I'll tell you right now, and neither is anyone I know."

"I just need information, Sir. No one believes it was you."

"You betcha! You know, I prefer my Winchester Model 70, like this right here..." He twisted his neck so that Stan could better see the tattoo. "I'm on the winning side with this one. You have to look at it pragmatically," he said with an unpleasantly callous tone. "Why do you think humans are history's most successful predators? The answer is simple: guns."

"Well, you could be right," Stan replied. "No animal stands a chance against a Winchester."

"Exactly! But if you want, if you *really* want a challenge, you can hunt with a spear. Have you heard about the exotic antelopes introduced in Texas? The populations exploded so crazily that the coyotes couldn't keep up."

"I've heard about it. Why do you ask?"

"See, there are these internet freaks who make videos of themselves climbing trees and killing a blackbuck or an antelope with a lance. They think it's great. Well, it makes sense to decimate the animals."

"We shouldn't confuse sense with fun. It does make sense to hunt if their population gets out of control, but not with lances. It's our own fault if an antelope species from India spreads like mad in an American state. All the more reason for us to use our brains instead of acting on instinct, no?"

Manchin scoffed. "You probably think you're an expert, ranger. But you have no idea about hunting; anyone can see that."

"Then go ahead, enlighten me!"

"If you hit the right spot with a spear or an arrow, it's actually the most humane method of all. The wound isn't big, for a start. It's a completely different story with a Winchester. But I prefer my Model 70. It has its... advantages."

"It was more of a disadvantage for the sea eagle," Stan commented dryly. "So, who kills a wolf with a javelin?"

"An extraordinary hunter, a unique hunter. Possibly dangerous. Probably dangerous, in fact. He must be a tough bastard, fast and strong and be able to climb, hide, aim well, and hit even better!"

Manchin stared at his empty coffee cup for a moment, then at Stan, forcing himself to smile a little. You could see a light flick on in the poacher's eyes, as if suddenly spotting a silver lining on the horizon. Could a deal be possible?

"That brilliant hunter," Manchin urged, "he's out there, isn't he? You want to find him, don't you? Listen, sir, if you want to track him down, take me on board! Get me out of here! I'll get him with my Winchester; you can be sure of that."

Stan gave him a disdainful look, stood up, and rang for the guard. "Thank you for the information, Mr. Manchin."

6

Professor Austin J. Walker strolled with a spring in his step across the modern campus of the University of Utah. His dark green linen shirt was unbuttoned wide, revealing a traditional riji with shell jewelry around his neck. He wore battered Blundstones and dark curls flowed from under his cowboy hat. Very few students thought he was an academic; most just saw a rather handsome globetrotter.

Those who knew him called him 'stockman,' a nickname left over from his days growing up as a rancher on his grandfather's Outback farm. Even today, he can hardly part with his Akubra, the legendary Australian felt hat made from rabbit hair. Walker loved his hat, his origins, and his slightly darker skin tone, and, as he liked to tell anybody who would listen, found it to be the best protection against sunburn.

Like so many immigrants from Scotland, his grandfather, Gerald Walker, had established himself as a cattle farmer in the Rangelands of northwestern Australia. Occasionally, he took his growing grandson on trips to the Kimberley, the sparsely populated northern region renowned for its endless wilderness, dramatic gorges, rugged mountain ranges, and deserted seashores. This is where Grandpa Gerald's first wife came from, as did the riji necklace which Walker never removed.

When the young Austin first saw the several thousand-year-old naturalistic rock paintings of the Indigenous Australians, his grandmother's ancestors, in Kimberley, he felt a deep, instinctive connection. The way he saw it, a great fortune had allowed him to be part of both Western and Indigenous cultures, which had been able to develop in isolation for over sixty thousand years. Only later did he realize that, thanks to this experience, he had also been gripped by paleoanthropology.

Austin was a free-spirited, well-loved child who grew up with siblings and friends on a ranch. He rode like the devil, made boomerangs, and mended fences. During vacations, he helped drive cattle from the paddocks to the ranch, went fly fishing, and conducted expeditions through the wild, vast backcountry. He was more interested in science and adventure than table soccer and video games.

Once he had come of age, he gladly fulfilled his father's wish and obtained a pilot's license for single-engine planes and helicopters, which fly the vast expanse of the Outback and keep livestock in check. But the day finally came when he had to admit to himself that the search for the origins of mankind captivated him far more than cattle breeding ever could. He wanted to understand the miracle of evolution and the ancient, animal-human being that still exists somewhere deep within us all. He dreamt of providing concrete, tangible answers to scholars in the humanities who never tire of dealing abstractly with that one immovable question: *Who am I?*

So, he trained another rancher to fly, packed his bags, and boarded a flight toward George Washington University. After earning his doctorate in paleoanthropology and returning to his homeland, he soon made headlines when his team of archaeologists succeeded in using wasps to determine the exact age of the famous Kimberley cave paintings that Austin had known since childhood.

Reporters would turn up at their family ranch morning after morning, each time asking how they did it. They might have expected a stern secrecy, but Austin was not about that; instead, he'd hand them a Victoria Bitter and tell them the whole story.

The Australian cave paintings' color pigments, he'd explain, are unsuitable for precise dating. The trick for his team of scientists was to date the components of wasp nests below and above the pigments instead, which was possible using the radiocarbon method. Once the age of the nests before and after the creation of the painting was known, the period in between—when the artwork was created—was at long last revealed.

The result was seventeen thousand three hundred years. The Kimberley stockman and his team had successfully identified Australia's oldest known rock paintings.

One year later, at thirty-six, he completed his habilitation, and Professor Austin Walker was appointed to the chair of Stone Age Cultures at the University of Utah.

7

Walker chose a rather unconventional approach to teaching. At the beginning of his short introductory lecture, he did not stand at the lectern. Instead, he sat down quietly on a table at the very back of the hall. The first-year students couldn't help but turn back to him, giggling and whispering to each other. Walker carefully placed his Akubra on the table to his left and an impressive skull on the other side. Satisfied that his backpack was now empty, he sat back and let the students observe.

The massive head grabbed most attention. It was elongated, with a low, receding forehead, powerful brow ridges, an oversized nostril, and a high jaw with large teeth. It seemed to stare at the students from its deep, shadowy eye sockets. Some enjoyed it; others found it unnerving. But all were captivated. Primal and gnarled, it stood out among the sterile furnishings of the modern lecture hall.

Walker's arrangement illustrated the perspective of paleoanthropology, which looks back to the tribal history of man. He enjoyed these moments of unadorned astonishment and waited patiently until silence had fallen once again. Then, he began with a simple question:

"Who are we?"

Silence.

"Well, on the surface," he continued, "we're the ones who whizz to university on our e-bikes, sit at plastic desks and watch Netflix until our eyes fall shut." Approving laughter followed as students recognized themselves in his description.

"You see, this all seems completely normal to us, but no other living being on this planet has ever done or would ever do these things. We are extraordinary and have become completely accustomed to this. We are shapers and change-makers responsible for the Anthropocene, the age named after us, Anthropos, the age in which we flip the big switches. Big deal, people!"

Silence again. This time, however, Walker sensed it was a silence borne of intrigue rather than confusion. He continued:

"The human impact on the environment is immense. Unfortunately, we are not changing our habitat for the better. We are building hospitals, fuel cells and data centers, sure, but we're also destroying the biological balance of nature, of which we are a part. We seem so entangled in our self-created, artificial world that we have lost the invisible bond to the miracle of life. The effects are catastrophic. We are transforming the climate right up to the Arctic, polluting the atmosphere, soil and oceans, and even managing to completely reshape the geography of our planet. Thousands of animal species are lost every year and, slowly, even the last of us is realizing that we are somehow in trouble."

That was sobering, and he knew it. Walker put on a mischievous smile, shook his head and said, "Bloody hell! I'm outta here!" The tension eased.

"Look, guys, if we want to pull ourselves out of this misery, a thorough self-reflection can't hurt. When we look back at where we came from and what we were, we can become a little more aware of who we are today. I assure you that there is much more to us than the anatomically modern human being stuck in the mire of daily life. Deep within us lies another, ancient creature connected to an equally ancient part of nature. Despite our ignorance, greed and destructiveness, it can be helpful to reflect on this creature and fathom the being that still lives in us today." Walker saw a student raise her hand.

"Is the essence of our ancestors still somehow recognizable or tangible?" she asked.

"A good question!" He stood up and took a step toward her. "What's your name? I'm Austin Walker. You can call me Walker; I don't mind."

"I'm Carol," the young woman replied. "Hey, Walker!" Some students laughed.

"The answer, Carol, is yes and no. No, because evolution can't be reversed—not yet, anyway. We are the humans of the twenty-first century, and this fellow here," Walker pressed his Akubra onto the ancient skull next to him, "He disappeared from the scene around thirty-five thousand years ago, which is unfortunate."

"That's a long time," Carol pondered. "So, how are we ever supposed to understand what he was really like, how he moved, what he thought... how he felt?"

"Seems impossible, doesn't it. But, believe me, we are well on the way to finding out. We have already solved many mysteries, but much more is out there to explore. That's what this course is all about: looking, learning, and understanding. The more we know, the more tangible things we get our hands on. A sixty-five-thousand-year-old cave painting is not just art; it tells us about the person who created it. Palaeoanthropology deals with forensics, like we're the detectives solving unexplained deaths dating back thousands of years. The tiniest clues might lead to a breakthrough. DNA extracted from fossilized bones gives us heaps of information about our ancestors, who were probably much smarter and more sensitive than previously assumed. Little by little, science is piecing together a picture of these fascinating creatures: how they lived, hunted and communicated; what they ate, invented and produced; and their abilities and weaknesses. And, of course, what they looked like. So-called paleoartists are now reconstructing realistic three-dimensional models for museums, universities, movies."

He paused for breath. The students were spellbound by what he had to say.

"The journey of discovery into our past is far from over. This program is your ticket to continue that journey, gain new insights about them and yourselves, make the intangible a little more tangible, and further complete this crazy puzzle called *Who are we?*"

An enthusiastic murmur vibrated through the lecture hall, and the students clapped and began to discuss with each other animatedly.

The professor had won them over.

8

Desperate and alone, Omu lit a small fire in a clearing deep in the forest. He only uses dry hardwood to keep the smoke to a minimum. Depressed, he chews on a lump of resin and checks his modest hunting equipment; his axe, knife and belt pouch are his only possessions. He makes the equipment himself and replaces it when necessary. The forest and the mountains give him everything he needs.

In addition to a stone axe, he made a hunting knife with a handle made of hard joint bone and a flint blade. Parts of the knife are tied together with dried, frayed and twisted animal sinew and glued with birch tar. His soft belt pouch made of weatherproof tanned deer hide contains meat for food, various medicinal herbs, an extremely sharp hand axe, a flint scraper for gutting prey, and tinder fungus—a tree fungus that is highly flammable when dry.

Omu's summer clothing, made of deerskin and buffalo hide, consists of a loincloth, leggings that reach the hips and attach to a belt, and tight-fitting, fur-lined moccasins. His reddish-haired upper body remains unclothed entirely.

The moccasins are sewn from a single piece of tanned deerskin and have an additional stiff leather sole. A suede strip is worked into the heel to make them easier to take off. A piece of fur is folded over the top and sewn on. It is used to tuck in the leggings. His neck is adorned with a chain made from the claws of a Kodiak.

Omu is experienced. He has a wealth of knowledge about his people and the wisdom of his ancestors. He knows how to hew stones, split bones, build pitfall traps, weave fish traps, and make sticky birch tar deep in the embers of the fire. He surveys the diverse plant kingdom, knows all the forest's roots, mosses and fungi, smells the resin under the bark, and evaluates the substances *trees give off. He appreciates the scent of edible flowers, finds strengthening fruits, identifies every medicinal herb and knows about their benefits.*

This knowledge is a gift from his fathers, a treasure he carries within him and draws on it whenever necessary. He was taught with his brothers and sisters; they all understand the same sounds, the voices that flow from their throats, their words that explain things and make the truth audible.

He had been tracking the wolf for almost a whole lunar cycle. He had often been close to it, but the elusive animal always escaped. The wolf was cunning and fast but weakened by wounds; it needed to rest often. It almost fell into Omu's hands several times.

Fear of death spurs on the driven, and a tenacious will drives the hunter. He always finds the wolf's trail. He reads the scent, recognizes every deceptive maneuver, interprets the calls of the birds that constantly betray the fugitive, and senses the dust spread by the watchful plants. So, he never lost him, but he was always unable to reach him.

He will never give up.

Omu smells the bobos, the high-headed people who took the wolf with them, and the symbol deep in its neck, which reveals the location of the hidden valley—the valley of his ancestors.

Wolves are howling in the distance, and he understands the message: There must be several packs of wolves that cannot escape some sort of captivity.

That's where the foolish thieves are.

That's where Omu's going, Omu's goal.

He is trembling. Exhaustion and pain have become his constant companions. Nevertheless, he will not turn back; he'll eat now, regain his strength, and stay here until his strength returns.

Tired, he digs a shallow hollow, finds moss and leaf mold, breaks up ferns and branches and creates a nest where he sleeps.

9

DNA carries the genetic information of every living organism; it is the blueprint of an individual, so to speak. However, the somewhat unstable DNA molecule breaks down into smaller and smaller fragments over time. If genetic information is to be extracted from old bones or teeth, science must reach its limits. It is no secret that, after thousands of years in the ground, bacteria and fungi colonize the human remains, and the genetic material of the microbes contaminates that of the bones. Under these conditions, it has not yet been possible to extract and analyze usable DNA from largely fossilized human fossils.

The Swede Svante Pääbo achieved a breakthrough not long after the arrival of the twenty-first century. He dedicated himself entirely to decoding the genome of Neanderthals, the legendary early man and the closest relative of humans living today. At the Max Planck Institute for Evolutionary Anthropology in Leipzig, he devised new approaches: his team worked under sterile conditions, developed more efficient extraction methods, and used complex computer programs to systematically assemble the DNA snippets from the ancient bones.

He was soon successful. Pääbo revealed to science a treasure trove of new clues about these bizarre, enigmatic creatures and—in turn—clues about ourselves. In 2010, he presented the first version of the Neanderthal genome. By 2014, he had succeeded in decoding it almost completely. By comparing it with our human DNA, the institute identified thirty thousand positions in which we differ. However, the public was particularly fascinated by the proof that a small percentage of Neanderthal DNA can be found in our own genetic material. In 2022, Pääbo was awarded the Nobel Prize for his findings.

Over the course of the last decade, new sequencing technologies have truly revolutionized genome research. Researchers are now able to study organic material in unprecedented depth and detail. Intelligent software makes it possible to digitize a DNA trace quickly and compare it with a database. The Utah University facility also offers next-generation sequencing services to its own research community and off-campus researchers.

Genetic analyses were an integral part of Walker's work. Conveniently, his new university's Department of Anthropology had provided a comfortable office right next to the Laboratory of Evolutionary Genetics. In this lab, he was assisted by an experienced chemistry assistant named Cindy Klein. At Utah University, molecular biology had already shed light on subjects like American population history, but Walker set his sights higher: he wanted to use it to reach back into the millions of years of human tribal past.

He had titled the lecture 'The Roots of Humanity.' Tomorrow evening, he would deliver it to his first-year students as a kind of compass for the year ahead. Walker assumed that most of them still didn't know much about paleoanthropology. Breaking down his own extensive knowledge into a few key points was, therefore, as necessary as it was tricky. So, he collected himself by brewing a strong rooibos tea, made himself comfortable on the couch, closed his eyes and started talking to himself:

"My dear ape Walker," he began, amused by his own address.

"Yes, that's right! You come from the ape family! But you prefer to call yourself Homo sapiens, a modern man.

We all grow up knowing that there is only one kind of human on earth: us, Homo sapiens. The existence of a second, alien form of human seems almost unimaginable. We feel far superior to the animal world; no other living creature can compete with us, neither for better nor for worse. We reach for the stars without any competition.

You grew up aware that you are the sole surviving representative of the human family tree. But remember, there was once another human species around—a whole human family!

If you look at the period of evolution, it was not so long ago that you shared your habitat with other representatives of the human genus. Just a few tens of thousands of years ago, a different human species suddenly stood before you: the Neanderthal. The creature probably frightened you because it was your closest relative, yet it seemed very peculiar. *Almost* like us... but not quite. Despite its human features, it seemed to be inhabited by an animal.

How did this come about?

Well, it's all due to a geographical separation that took place over some five hundred thousand years—an incredibly long separation followed by a brilliant reunion.

To understand this, let's go back two million years.

Based on everything we know today, it was at this time that some clans of our common ancestor, Homo erectus, first migrated from their African nursery to Eurasia. This is shown by 1.85-million-year-old finds in Georgia and 1.2-million-year-old excavations in Spain. Homo erectus itself emerged on the African continent from the earliest representatives of the genus Homo, including Australopithecus, which already walked upright, and Homo rudolfensis, perhaps the first hominin to use stone tools.

The skull of Homo erectus is very similar to that of a gorilla, but its body is less so. Even when compared to us; it has a more primitive shape. The elongated skull has a very low forehead, a powerful, continuous bulge over the eyes, a broad nasal bridge and widely spaced eye sockets. Like the snout of a monkey, the dental arches of the upper and lower jaws protrude from the face. We call this form of dentition of some vertebrates *prognathism*.

Homo erectus, you might already know, means 'upright man'. If you like, he is the forefather of mankind because, like us, he walks upright, creates tools, and masters fire. He was also the first to use targeted hunting as a vital element for securing his food supply. His brain volume is still considerably smaller than ours, but when another wave of immigration from Africa to Eurasia occurred around six hundred thousand years ago, the brain was already a third larger. They developed fast.

Some of these early human ancestors remained in Africa, while others reached Eurasia. Once the geographical separation was complete, different evolutionary developments took place. While the Homo populations that remained in Africa developed into Homo sapiens, Homo naledi, and other Homo species over hundreds of thousands of years, the clans in Eurasia mutated into other primitive human forms: via Homo heidelbergensis, they mutated into Neanderthals in Europe, Denisova man in Asia, Flores man in Indonesia and Luzon man in the Philippines. So, you can see that several different representatives of the genus Homo existed simultaneously, both in Africa, their cradle, and in Eurasia.

Now, here's one of the most interesting parts. The dating of fossil remains in 2017 shows that Homo naledi probably coexisted with Homo sapiens in southern Africa three hundred thousand years ago. Two researchers made the discovery in the Rising Star cave system near Johannesburg in 2013. They penetrated a previously unexplored chamber through a breathtakingly narrow cave passage. The floor was littered with thousands of fossilized bones. Two years later, it became clear that Homo naledi is a separate species of the genus Homo, weighing only around eighty-eight pounds. Their average height is four foot six, and their anatomy is a strange mixture of primitive and modern features. The primitive features are their ape-like shoulders, dentition, and tiny brain, which are slightly larger than a chimpanzee.

However, they prove that a small brain is not synonymous with poor thinking skills. Homo naledi walked upright, controlled fire and buried relatives in graves. Most impressively, scientists found many symbols engraved into the walls. These three-hundred-thousand-year-old, deeply engraved hashtag-like cross-hatchings and other geometric shapes are the oldest known symbol structures."

Walker sipped his tea. He saw images of the evolution unfold in his mind.

"Neanderthals are genetically nothing like you, Walker. They differ from you more than any ethnic group living today differs from any other. Very peculiar is his bulging skull, the upper part of which is almost without a forehead at all. Compared to ours, his head is probably as indestructible as a roughly carved block of wood. With his expansive chest, broad pelvis and stocky, shorter legs, a Neanderthal has a heavy, compact appearance despite his smaller stature. His skeleton is extremely robust, and his body is muscular and massive. These, as you might imagine, are significant advantages in a northern climate that frequently and abruptly went from warm to cold extremes.

The Flores and Luzon people are entirely different. Somewhere around eight hundred thousand years ago, a few Homo erectus crossed the seas to reach the islands of Luzon in the Philippines and Flores in Indonesia. Geographically isolated, they evolved into true hunter-gatherers, growing to hardly more than three feet tall, a phenomenon that has something to do with so-called island dwarfism. Due to the scarcity of food, the body size of some species can decrease significantly over generations in remote land areas. For example, dwarf elephants once lived on Sicily, dwarf mammoths on Crete, and even tiny hippos on some Mediterranean islands. They have become extinct in the past millennia. A small endemic subspecies of reindeer still lives on the island of Spitsbergen."

He pictured the students melting into a collective 'awww' at the image of these creatures. After a large gulp of coffee, he continued.

"Homo floresiensis, also known as the hobbit, has oversized feet and very long arms in relation to its small body size. Even today, inhabitants of the regions report tiny forest dwellers who live in, with, and from nature without affecting their habitat. The even tinier Luzon people with their strange skulls and curved toes, which suggest that they spent a lot of time in trees, are also thought to be extinct, but are they really?"

This fact particularly fascinated Walker. Like some other scientists, he believed such creatures might have survived to this day, living quietly as invisible hunters somewhere in the depths of the primeval forest.

10

Omu is awake in his nest. Bright sunlight flickers through the rustling leaves of the treetops. He had a dream:

His clan sat wailing around the large fire. The sacred spear of the leader, his father, stood in the embers. But without a point, the spear was useless. The shaft was missing its head.

Omu was startled and fell into a deep ravine. Lying on the ground, he was enveloped in complete darkness. A wolf approached. Omu could sense its presence.

"Why are you chasing me?" the wolf asked with long, tired confusion.

"I am hunting you because my people are in great danger."

"I will not harm your people."

"I know that. But there is a secret in you. The great secret of my people."

"I won't reveal it."

"But the bobos will tell when they find it." Omu grabbed the back of the wolf's neck. "This is where it is. This is where the secret is!"

At that moment, the wolf snapped, and Omu woke up.

The air is becoming warm. The hunter rises from his nest, stretches, and yawns through his wide, yellow-toothed mouth. He knows that sleep paints confused pictures that play with reality, but he knows too that life is reflected in every dream.

The secret of his clan is true: the weapon with the artfully crafted bone head. For generations, it and its symbols have been their focus. Anyone who knows the symbols will find access to the hidden valley, their place of refuge.

The brothers and sisters have always gathered around their treasure, danced around it and murmured:

"Where the spear is, so are the people; where the people are, the spear reveals itself."

According to custom, only those who kill a wolf with this unique weapon can become a leader. Following his father's death, Omu has to prove himself capable of this. So, he set off, sneaking through the countryside for days in search of tracks.

He chose a beautiful, proud wolf. A creature in his prime, neither sick nor weak. He was strong and able to defend himself, and Omu knew it would take days to find him. So, he made himself a temporary shelter high up in the mountains—somewhere he could eat, sleep, and prepare for the hunt. He collected colorful rocks and ore, from which he extracted the pigments he used to paint pictures on the cave's wall. In his solitude, he blew his flute and knotted a necklace of feather ornaments for Kela, his chosen wife.

In Omu's world, animals are only killed as needed; no animal dies in vain. Everyone takes what they need, no more; that's what Mother Nature wants because everything is part of her precious whole, without which there is no survival. When the wolf is killed, it gives itself up: its meat, its fur, its fangs, its bones and its sinews. The wolf's death also proves the strength and wisdom of the new leader.

On the morning of the fifth day, Omu spotted a powerful animal from his position, high in a tree. It appeared like a ghost because its robust, heavy physique and strong bite reminded him of the wolves in the elders' stories. Old Watka called them 'ice wolves.' She still had a skull among her belongings and told the story of the ancestors these animals accompanied on their march across the great, cold land bridge.

Omu interpreted his encounter with an ice wolf as a great sign. His fate would be sealed.

Everything happened in an instant. The wolf was alert and quick. Omu hit it from the tree. As the spearhead dug into the vertebrae of its neck, the animal had already started to leap. The force of the penetrating javelin caused it to somersault in the air. In full spin, the long wooden shaft hit a stone and broke.

Before Omu could swing himself down, the ice wolf had gotten back on its legs and made a dart for safety. The spearhead lodged against its neck vertebra, held fast without piercing. The wolf survived and was able to escape.

Omu roared in despair. It couldn't have been any worse. If he had missed his prey, he would have come across another one. But now, the wolf had taken his clan's most sacred possession. The hunter had no choice but to give chase and follow the fresh scent through the forest. He soon merged with nature and used his ancient senses. There was only one solution: he had to catch up with the wolf and hunt it down.

He embarked on his mission equipped only with the bare essentials. But at only seventeen summers old, he was young, agile, and persistent. He soon felt the proximity to the fleeing animal and knew that the animal sensed him too. That was how it had to be. Maintaining this connection was Omu's only chance.

As dusk fell, he approached the injured, exhausted ice wolf. Then, unexpectedly, a foolish horse rider appeared. The bobo man had a rifle and was getting ready to kill the wolf and take it with him. Omu stepped in, grabbed a pinecone, and hurled it at the horse's hindquarters from his cover. The horse reared up, and the wolf escaped.

The hunt continued. Fear drove the fleeing animal, but Omu kept finding its trail. Many days and nights passed before that night.

Omu listens. His pulse hammered against his broad neck like a river stone caught in a current. Yes, he fears the bobos, the high-headed people to whom he is closer than ever before. But the fate of his people lies in his hands. He must regain possession of the spearhead before a stranger recognizes what it reveals. No one is allowed to look at it.

There it is, where the bobos live. Where the captive wolves howl.

Walker's cell phone buzzed. He opened a distressing message from archaeologist Keryn Walshe. Vandals had ruined a wonderful piece of prehistoric songline artwork by Indigenous Australians, one of the last of its kind. The site of the horror was Koonalda Cave. The narrow-mindedness of these barbarians could not be surpassed. Whatever destructive mining and climate change had left of the place of worship now seemed irrecoverably lost.

"Don't look now, but this is a den of death," read the cynical, carved inscription of the destroyers.

Walker was highly familiar with this site's cultural and historical backgrounds. The twenty-two-thousand-year-old artistic legacies in the South Australian cave are famous testimonies to the Whale Dreaming songlines. Engravings and graphic symbols of Aboriginal people can be seen on the vast cave walls.

Walker's grandmother still knew some of the songlines that comprised the Aboriginal creation story. From time to time, she repeated the mystical words and explained that songlines are sung maps that point to geographical features and sacred sites.

As hunter-gatherers, the Aboriginal clans used their habitat sustainably. Instead of overexploiting an area, destroying their food base and damaging their sacred sites, they moved to another location while allowing old hunting grounds to regenerate. Making their way through these vast unknown realms, the wanderers had nothing close to the accuracy of online maps or written travel guides. But they knew the magical songs— the songlines of their ancestors who once roamed these lands. They told them about cultural and geographical features of the new regions: river courses, mountain ranges, game populations, and occult sites of their ancestors. They were, in essence, sung guides that enabled people to find their way through the vastness of Australia, and, over thousands of years, helped them to survive.

Walker felt anger and despair. To demolish such a silent testimony to a peaceful culture was utter madness. It seemed scandalous that nothing had been done to protect the site beforehand.

His phone beeped again. He yawned, stretched, and opened the new message. It contained pictures of a car accident: a destroyed Toyota Prius, a wolf in a pool of blood beside it, and an attractive woman in a green jumpsuit who resembled the Australian actress Margot Robbie. A close-up showed an injury to the neck of the dead wolf, and another showed the front and back of a distinctive spearhead. The caption read:

"Prof. A. Walker—What is this? Urgent!"

Walker almost choked on his tea. Frowning, he leaned in, eyes fixed, utterly captivated by the picture on the screen.

"That's impossible!"

Hardly anyone knew more about Stone Age weapons than he did. Yet, even for him, this object was unique. It was not in any museum, and it certainly had no place in a wolf's neck. He zoomed in. The projectile point, probably the head of a spear, looked flawless. Had it been restored, or was it a replica? In any case, he had never seen anything like it. On one side of the double-edged head were intricate engravings that looked like mysterious signs or symbols—highly unusual, and highly intriguing.

At last, Walker's eyes flicked to the sign-off that concluded the message: *Stan Hardy, Utah Department of Conservation.*

The name didn't trigger any recognition, so the professor called him right back. Their conversation was brief and matter-of-fact. Stan gave him a short and friendly explanation of the accident and mentioned

Lilly Feron's wolf park, where the deceased animal had been examined. Walker asked where the spear tip was.

"It's on its way to you, Professor. We'd like you to take a closer look at this thing."

"Sure, of course. These kinds of artifacts fall within my area of expertise. And from what I've seen so far, to be honest, I'm amazed."

"So are we. Who *does* that? Who hunts a wolf with a throwing device? Maybe you'll find out something."

"Have you already examined the weapon for DNA?"

"The guys in the lab say that part of it is made of bone, but its DNA looks unusual."

"Unusual?"

"Yes. They mean it's kind of human, but something about it is different, so, I guess… not human?"

"So, which is it, human or animal?"

Short silence.

"Neither. No idea. Kind of strange."

"This entire weapon seems strange to me, Mr. Hardy."

"Just like the wolf that was hunted with it. Maybe you should talk to Ms. Feron. She knows her stuff. She's playing a guessing game just like we are."

"Good, I'll get in touch with her. Do you have her number?"

"Yes. You'll receive the delivery tomorrow morning. It's addressed to you personally. One more thing: please treat it confidentially. This is an active and high-priority case. Ms. Feron's contact information is enclosed."

"I see. I'll let you know as soon as I learn anything."

"Thank you for your time. Good night, Professor."

"Walker, just Walker."

His head was spinning. Stan's words left him even more bewildered than before.

12

Omu needs food before he sets off. Determined, he searches for crab apples and sea buckthorn, and on the way accumulates a collection of king oyster mushrooms, blackberries, fresh broad plantain, grass seeds and dandelions and digs up edible roots to store in his bag. He takes just as much as he needs— nothing more.

When Omu is hungry and thirsty, a predator awakens in him. His senses sharpen, and his unbridled strength is unleashed. He hears, sees, smells, and feels the earth, the rock, the air, the water, the whole forest, and all the animals in it. He is then part of the wilderness and entirely in his element.

The jay's hoarse cry shows him prey. He scents it against the wind and approaches it agilely and silently. When he recognizes the outline of the young roebuck in the bushes, he pauses for a moment, takes a deep breath, and collects himself. Then, he hurls the stone axe at his victim with full force and enormous accuracy. The short, heavy axe makes its way through the air, hissing softly, smashing through the underbrush on its flat, curved trajectory before its razor-sharp stone head digs into the unsuspecting buck's temple.

In no time, the hunter has broken open the prey and removed the best pieces: fresh liver, raw muscle meat, and the nutritious stomach. He devours some on the spot until his belly bulges, wraps another portion in leaves, and stows it away. The rest is left to the forest.

Invigorated, Omu resumes the chase, gliding through the landscape as if intoxicated. In his mind, he transforms into a fox, a swallow, a fish, and a moth. He dodges the bobos' paths, avoids every source of noise and gradually inches closer to his goal: the captured wolves.

It may be his last journey, but he is ready for anything. Turning back is impossible. Without the spearhead, he cannot return to his people or face Kela, his chosen wife. If the relic is lost, he is lost; if it falls into the wrong hands, his entire people are lost. That is not an option.

The spearhead bears the secret symbol that reveals where his people are hiding. If a hunter loses track of his position, the symbol shows him the way from the three giant larches to the lake. No one but his clan knows the hidden valley exists, and no one else gets to see it or enter it. It has been like this from the very beginning.

The falling water hides the entrance. The rocky cave offers protection and cover. A dense, evergreen coniferous forest covers the shielded habitat. Only there, cut off from the world, has it been possible to survive since the beginning. Bobo people once came into the area. But they were unwise, loud, and visible to everyone because they had long since forgotten how to be wild. Omu spotted them immediately and followed them. Their colorful clothing shone brightly, and they puffed under their heavy backpacks.

He made himself invisible to them, became part of the forest, merged with it like the wind with the mist, like the fox deep in the den and the bird's nest in the dense grass. Omu merged with the stream, the shadow, the leaf, and the earth. Making certain that he was neither seen nor heard, he trudged on into the mountains.

The ice wolf took the spearhead with him, and the bobos took the ice wolf with them. Now, Omu is close to them. He will take what he has and proceed prudently, carefully, quietly, and wisely.

The day passes by. The night awaits.

13

Walker slept fitfully. So far, he had only seen Stan's photos, but there was something unfathomable about them. In the morning, he was restless. He could hardly wait for the shipment to arrive. When it finally did, it took all his powers of restraint not to greet the burly DHL courier with a hug.

The professor carried the small yellow and red package into the kitchenette, armed himself with rubber gloves and a mask, and carefully opened it with his Leatherman folding knife. Out came the artifact, wrapped in absorbent cotton and plastic and accompanied by a hastily written note disclosing Lilly Feron's contact information.

As the projectile lay on the fresh towel before him, Walker spontaneously thought of experimental archaeology, a discipline where ancient tools and devices are painstakingly rebuilt and tried out in the field. *Was this also a reconstructed object?* There was no doubt that it was particularly exquisite, something he recognized immediately.

During his studies at George Washington University, the field hoe—man's oldest agricultural tool—was the subject of his field experiment. Despite its simplicity, the hoe is essential. It has been used for thousands of years by almost all people to cultivate the soil. As a student, Walker was interested in discovering if Neanderthals could have made hoes to loosen the soil.

Scientists place the beginning of agriculture in the Neolithic period around twelve thousand years ago, long after the Neanderthals had disappeared from the scene. However, early humans were already using similar techniques to make sophisticated spears and javelins. So, the idea came to Walker: why not hoes, too?

For the field test, the budding professor carefully fashioned a hoe exactly like those used by anatomically modern humans in the Neolithic period. The reconstruction incorporated all his knowledge about the manufacturing techniques and materials of the time such that the reconstructed hoe should be indistinguishable from the original.

He then produced a similar hoe for comparison, using joining techniques that the Neanderthals had already mastered and materials that were available to early humans at the time. Once completed, he conducted various practical experiments. In each test, he learned about the efficiency and stability of his device. After trying it out himself, he couldn't help but think—Neanderthals must have known how to work the soil. That skill alone could have been the spark that made farming possible.

As unique as it was, the spear's tip fell within Walker's field of expertise. And it raised questions. On the surface, it was about poaching. But why did the hunter use the finest art and such precious, unique materials? The smoothly ground, barbed, double-edged bone spearhead was the size of a baby's hand. The hafting, or how the shaft and projectile point were joined, required considerable expertise and dexterity.

Walker recognized that the manufacturer used several sophisticated techniques to join the tip to the wooden handle. The spearhead was stuck to the shaft in a so-called socket and was attached with loops and sticky earth pitch, which was a complex procedure. The conical socket was also designed as an incomplete perforation, which made it possible to replace each worn-out projectile with a new one. The craftsman had bound and glued both parts so tightly that the wooden shaft would break on impact rather than the intermediate piece because it was technically so sophisticated and difficult to produce! To Walker, it seemed that methods from different eras of cultural history had been intelligently combined in the same object. The most exciting thing, however, was the artistic value of the spearhead. Not at all in keeping with experimental archaeology, there was a highly peculiar, fine engraving on one of the flattened sides. The motif, roughly one and a half square inches in size, stood out on the bright, smooth surface. He picked up a magnifying glass and examined the tiny image. Its breathtaking detail looked like a miniature map of symbols and structures.

The artist intricately engraved the symbols with a sharp, pointed instrument. *But why?* The idea of such a masterfully crafted javelin being used for the unauthorized hunting of wild animals seemed downright absurd. Despite his euphoria, Walker was once again struck by a queasy feeling, the same feeling he had when Stan spoke of the "strange DNA" in the material. He searched hard for explanations, but nothing fit together.

Finally, the wolf expert Lilly Feron, whom he had seen, and liked, in the photos, came to mind. He felt the urge to talk to her. In a fit of inspiration, he searched Yelp for a restaurant he supposed a woman like Lilly might enjoy, dialed her number, and arranged to meet for what he hoped would be an informative conversation. He carefully repacked the artifact and carried it to the neighboring lab for forensic testing.

Though the lab was teeming with staff and students in similar work clothes, Cindy Klein was impossible to miss. Her short, neon green hair stood out among the employees.

"What luck, I love green. I recognized you right away. Many thanks to your hairdresser!"

She liked him because he was competent, charming, and funny. "I'll take care of it. How did the lecture go?"

"They tarred and feathered me.... No, it was fun with the students. But, Cindy, could I talk to you in private for a moment?"

"Any time, Professor."

The chemistry lab assistant slid a pallet of test tubes into a compartment and strolled with him to an office in the back of the lab. Walker closed the door gently, grinned at her engagingly and handed her the small package.

"I bet my life and my riji shell necklace that this will blow you away!"

Smiling sheepishly and a little self-consciously, she took it. "What's this?" She seemed happily surprised, almost as if she were receiving a gift.

"Something that could one day end up in the National Museum of Natural History."

"Where did you get it?"

"That's not important for now. I was asked to be discreet. Do you trust me?"

"Absolutely, Professor Walker."

"It's all about the material; apparently, it's bone. But from which creature and how old? That's the question that's left people—smart people—confused. But I suspect a forensic genetic examination will certainly help us with that."

She smiled warmly at him again. "If you like, I'll get started right away."

"You're a gem!"

After a few tense hours, the results were available.

14

As he entered the parking lot, it occurred to Walker that the Tuscany on the city's east side seemed almost a little too romantic for a formal lunch with a pretty biologist he had never met. Still, since Lilly Feron was also keenly interested in the strange incident, she accepted right away.

Inside, she was already sitting at a white table in the secluded restaurant garden. The early afternoon sun bathed the Mediterranean ambience in bright orange tones. Many guests came from the Old Mill golf course to the east or Knudsen Park to the south.

Walker recognized her immediately—not many women bear such a striking resemblance to Margot Robbie. He waved discreetly, dutifully removed his Akubra and strolled casually through the busy restaurant toward her.

"Hello, Ms. Feron, I'm Walker, Austin Walker."

He liked that she stood up and shook his hand firmly, as well as her unadorned, natural manner.

"Lilly. Good to meet you."

She was still wearing her worn green overalls with the Feron Wolf Park logo and dusty trekking boots, which probably attracted a few irritated looks from the restaurant's regular clientele. Walker, however, found it distinctly charming.

"Thank you for taking the time to see me." Worrying this might have sounded too formal, so he quickly added, "I had no idea how delightful this restaurant is."

"Yes, it is indeed. It would have been my choice, too."

She didn't need to mention that she knew it well. She allowed him the joy of discovery. Walker kindly adjusted her chair and sat himself opposite her.

"Please excuse my tardiness. Everything is coming at me at once. Two days ago, I arrived in Salt Lake City and was immediately confronted with this strange object. And in a few hours, I'll be giving the first evening lecture of my paleoanthropology course."

"I understand."

A waitress came over and Walker confidently ordered a mixed salad, a cheese platter with ciabatta bread and pesto, plus two glasses of Vermentino and mineral water. Lilly immediately trusted the dark, curly-haired Australian. She waited until the waitress had moved away a little, then sought his gaze, leaned over the table, and said, "The wolf is a specimen of a prehistoric population."

Walker sat motionless as he let the sentence sink in. The spearhead also seemed prehistoric. Understandably, though, Lilly was primarily concerned with the wolf. So, he also replied in a whisper: "That's certainly fantastic. Especially for an expert like yourself, right?"

"It sure is."

"Are you sure about the classification?"

"I examined the animal thoroughly in my clinic. The overall impression speaks for itself. It is undoubtedly a Beringian wolf and officially long extinct. The animals lived on the land bridge between Siberia and Alaska during the Great Glaciation."

"In the Pleistocene, in Beringia, hence the name."

"Right. And far into the Holocene, apparently *very* far. More precisely, right up to the present day, it seems."

"You don't know where and how this wolf survived?"

"He's traveled a long way south. Almost four hundred miles."

"You know his origin?"

"Sort of. Someone claimed to have seen such an animal east of Salmon River only three weeks ago. My intern researched it. Doesn't look like it was given a whole lot of attention at the time. The man's name is Stolin. Frank Stolin. Apparently, he works for Painted Rocks State Park in Montana… and probably traps on the side, no doubt."

"A trapper, then, someone who's after furs. How nice!"

Lilly sighed. "Yes, very nice. I suspect our wolf was wounded there about three weeks ago—around the time it was spotted."

"Montana, Idaho… I know Coopers Ferry on the Salmon River."

"Have you ever been there?"

"No, but people of the Ice Age certainly did. An excavation team found tons of primitive tools there and even the remains of an Ice Age horse. Over many thousands of years, Stone Age people found their way to this site—Homo sapiens, of course. The archaeologists identified a fourteen-thousand-year-old hearth. A fascinating place in a fairly deserted mountain region." A momentary wave of self-consciousness flashed over him. "Sorry, kinda nerdy I knew. This is just, well, my *thing.*"

"Not at all. Deserted indeed. This kind of wilderness hardly exists anywhere else. One of the few remaining areas that have been left truly alone."

"Oh, but there's still a lot of wilderness out there," Walker replied cautiously.

Lilly looked at him. "We're not talking about Australia anymore, Mr. Walker," she said gently and confidently.

"You know where I'm from?"

"That's a riji, isn't it?"

Walker grabbed his necklace. Lilly grinned in good humor. He smiled back and winked mischievously.

"From my *ancestors*."

She nodded appreciatively. There was something attractive about him. So as not to seem embarrassed, she carried on.

"It's unmistakable. The colonization of the United States seems unstoppable: fracking in nature reserves, mass tourism, and authorities that want to control every nook and cranny. The unspoiled wilderness will soon be a thing of the past."

Their food and wine arrived.

"We still have forty percent of the country. An area the size of India is completely untouched Down Under."

"You are to be envied for that."

Walker raised his glass. "To the wilderness!"

They clinked glasses. Lilly didn't necessarily see herself as an environmental activist. But she was aware of the urgency and advocated her position emphatically whenever the opportunity arose.

"Along with Canada, America is the largest country in the world. A boundless expanse, you might think. But there are roads and oil and gas pipelines almost everywhere. That's a problem when protecting endangered wild animals, as it disrupts their migration routes."

Walker poured her a glass, ate, and listened with keen interest.

"If I remember the figures correctly," said Lilly, "there are over three million seven hundred thousand miles of public roads in the USA... and that's not including private roads, service roads, and off-road vehicle paths. Add to those two-and-a-half million miles of oil and natural gas pipelines and about one hundred and fifty-five thousand miles of high-voltage transmission lines and, well, I would call that a landscape cut up into bite-sized pieces!"

"I agree with you," Walker replied tactfully. "And what about Salmon River?"

Lilly's expression brightened. The professor thought she looked adorable, and worked hard to stifle the wave of attraction that he felt flush his gaze.

"That, Mr. Walker, is one of nature's last refuges—the original America, you could say. Over two million hectares of paradise located between Oregon, Montana, and Idaho. There, real wilderness still exists. You'll be hard-pressed to find any roads at all. Salmon River carves its way into a gorge that is deeper in places than the Grand Canyon. There are impassable mountains with vertical rock faces. Some sections are simply impenetrable. A perfect habitat for endangered species such as mountain lions, wolverines..."

"...and Beringian wolves!"

Lilly grinned at this idea as she spread pesto on ciabatta bread and added crumbs of goat cheese. "Yes, that would be great for this particular species and sensational for science!"

Walker became thoughtful. He allowed himself a moment of silence and then muffled, "The wolf, Miss. Feron... he was hunted... with an incredible weapon."

"Uh-huh. What kind of weapon? Were you able to find out anything about it?"

"If you say the rediscovery of such a wolf is sensational, Lilly, I believe you. And let me tell you, the same goes for the spearhead that wounded him. I know a lot about prehistoric weapons, but I've *never* seen anything like this one."

"And this unusual thing was in a Beringian wolf, of all things. That can hardly be a coincidence." She sipped her Vermentino thoughtfully, letting its lime and grapefruit notes settle on her tongue.

Walker could barely tear himself away from her emerald eyes until his phone buzzed. He answered the call. "Cindy!"

Lilly concentrated on her salad while the professor was subjected to Cindy's excitable flood of words, barely audible to her through the speaker. A minute later, when she saw his face, she stopped chewing.

He was stunned, repeating, "No, no, no," and shaking his head. He spoke in a broken voice: "Are you sure? Okay... Cindy, please... it has to stay between us. It *must*. Thank you."

He dropped the phone onto the table and slumped deeper into the garden chair. The professor sat there, pale and distraught, and Lilly felt sorry for him.

Walker's next words came only after what felt like an eternity, as if in a trance: "The genetic material. The DNA of the bone from which the projectile was made. Cindy analyzed it."

"What's wrong with the DNA? Is something wrong?"

"Well, the lab technician compared it with data sets from the Max Planck Institute for Evolutionary Anthropology in Leipzig. Perhaps you've heard of the Neanderthal genome project?"

"Didn't they decode the genetic material of these early humans?"

"That's right. Cindy couldn't believe it."

Lilly leaned far over the table again, as close to the professor as possible. "*What* couldn't she believe, Walker?"

"Neanderthals! The head of the spear... it's made of bone... bone from a Neanderthal!" he whispered.

"But how? It can't be. The thing wasn't fossilized. It wasn't *that* old."

"Cindy says only a few decades."

"But Neanderthals are long extinct."

"Just like the Beringian wolves."

"Possible contamination?"

"She rules it out. She's sure of it."

"An error in the calibration?"

"Hardly possible."

"I can't believe it!" Lilly was now wholly perplexed.

Walker wanted to laugh but couldn't; it got stuck in his throat. He could only shake his head. He put his face in his hands, exhausted. It seemed like the Dreamtime, the mythology of his Australian ancestors, had at long last caught up with him.

"I think I'm losing my mind." He looked around and made sure no one else could hear him. "They're alive! Somewhere out there in the wilderness. They still exist today."

Lilly also put her hand over her mouth to muffle her emotions. Then she said, somewhat composed: "And I even have an idea as to the location—where the wolf was."

"Quite possibly."

Could that be? He pulled himself together and forced himself to look at the matter objectively and critically.

"You know, Lilly, Neanderthals in America .... For science, that's a taboo. They colonized Europe, the Middle East, Central Asia, and western Siberia. And that's it. Conventional wisdom is that they never set foot on this continent. There is zero evidence for this; there are *zero* archaeological finds."

"But now it seems that they do exist."

Walker beamed at her. "You know, I've been thinking about this question for years. I often had to step back because there were only theories, nothing solid. Generally, a recognized expert shouldn't stray too far from the conventional wisdom in public. Otherwise, he runs the risk of being labelled a conspiracy theorist and risking his reputation."

"I'm not the public, Professor. Just an interested biologist."

"And what a biologist!"

He found himself wondering if she had someone, while she couldn't stop questioning why he captivated her so completely. He was thrilling—alive in every sense. For what felt like forever, they held each other's gaze, an invisible current passing between them; to resist would have been useless.

Lilly was the first to regain control of her emotions: "Let me get this straight, Professor. We, modern humans, made it this far thousands of years ago... but the Neanderthals didn't?"

"Because this form of human, according to scientific consensus anyway, no longer existed at the time of America's colonization. Treatises are written in black and white: our cousins, the Neanderthals, died out around thirty to forty thousand years ago. The Denisovans could have survived in New Guinea until fifteen thousand years ago. Then, they, too, disappeared."

Lilly recognized the turmoil in his expression, so she tried all the harder to put things into perspective.

"Modern man, Homo sapiens, only reached North America after these early humans had already disappeared from the face of the Earth."

"Correct. But there are reasons to doubt it. When and how anatomically modern humans, also known as Cro-Magnons, first emigrated to America has long been debated. The only certain thing is that America was the last landmass on Earth to be colonized."

"About eighteen thousand years ago, right?"

"Much earlier. In 2021, my colleagues in New Mexico made an incredible discovery. In the Tularosa Basin, near the shore of an ancient lake in White Sands National Park, they found human footprints that were twenty-three thousand years old. So, humans reached North America *much* earlier."

"Across the Bering Strait, right?" said Lilly, like a clever schoolchild eager to impress her teacher. "My father told me that Beringia was a paradisiacal tundra grassland back then, home to huge herds of animals and, of course, predators like Beringian wolves."

"That's right, the hunters followed the great herds and crossed the land bridge from the old world to the new, from eastern Siberia to Alaska. Today, Beringia lies one hundred and sixty-four feet below the water's surface. But we know it was passable repeatedly over the last one hundred and forty thousand years, either because global sea levels receded or because a layer of ice covered it."

Lilly listened patiently. He was inspiring, and she liked him. Walker sensed this, and things continued to bubble out of him.

"What is particularly exciting for me is that twenty-three thousand years ago, when the footprints were created, two huge ice sheets made North America inhospitable to life. Therefore, migration south from Alaska was unlikely. The ancestors of the people in the Tularosa Basin must have crossed the Bering Bridge before the glaciers formed... we're talking more than twenty-six thousand years ago. Quite a few experts assume that the first migrations could have occurred over thirty-five thousand years ago."

"... when Neanderthals still existed."

"Correct. Eleven thousand five hundred years ago, an ice-free corridor opened up within the Americas, making a southward migration from Alaska possible."

"But first, they must have covered the long distance to Eastern Siberia."

"If Homo sapiens could do it, Homo neanderthalensis could do it. His physique was made for a cold climate. We already know that he made it as far as Siberia. In 2022, scientists found the remains of an entire Neanderthal clan in the Siberian Chagyrskaya Cave near Mongolia, high up in the mountains. From there, hunters could overlook a vast, paradisiacal plain where herds of large wild animals grazed. Remains of stone tools and bison bones bear witness to this. And if the Neanderthals made it this far, why not as far as Beringia? They had warm clothing, and from the southwest, they may have been under pressure from the spread of modern man."

"They moved to the northeast."

"Possibly. If there was water to cross in places, that wasn't a problem. Sixty thousand years ago, people from the Stone Age could most likely colonize Australia only as seafarers on rafts, for example. And if the distance was manageable, they swam. They swam well. We know this from a population that lived in Italy around one hundred thousand years ago. Their deformed ear bones show that they suffered from swimmer's ear. They dived deep to look for shellfish; they ate the fish and used the shells to make tools."

"You mean something like *this*?" Lilly stretched out her arm and pertly poked the riji around Walker's neck with her index finger. Then, she slapped the table decisively with the flat of her hand. "So, there we have it! We seriously have to ask ourselves if these creatures are extinct. Everything is falling into place, and, as of today, there's even circumstantial evidence."

Walker called a waiter and indicated he wanted to pay. "The Beringian wolf may lead us to a lost human form," he whispered.

Lilly grinned sweetly at him. "There's only one way for us to find out."

There was no time to lose. Walker put on his Akubra and adjusted it. "Lilly, do you know how to ride?"

15

The matter was far too important to hesitate for even a moment. From the Tuscany, they drove to the nearest mall to buy supplies for a multi day trek. Then, they went to Feron Wolf Park, where a whole arsenal of equipment filled one of the storerooms: high shelves were piled with gear for workers, equipment for scientific expeditions, outdoor clothing, measuring instruments, tools, specialized cameras, equestrian equipment and much more. They put together what they needed, and Lilly was pleased that her father's trekking boots fit Walker perfectly.

"I knew they'd be your size! He is said to have been one of the best in his field and enjoyed a high reputation as a wolf whisperer. He often said he was following the call of the wild. I think he would have liked to come with us on this trip."

"I would have loved that, too."

Lilly dialed a number and winked at Walker. "Hi, Uncle Miller, it's Lilly... is your baby ready to go? Yes, I need you... Great! Great! Yes, the wilderness is calling again! Or rather, the salmon are calling... To Montana... Yes, Montana! Yes, right, it's not exactly around the corner. You know, Painted Rocks Lake. Can you land on it...? Yes, tonight, if possible...? Just a few days... Well, at dawn at the jetty on the Great Salt Lake... okay... okay... Fill up the tank, Uncle Miller. See you later."

"That was fast," said Walker, visibly impressed.

"An old friend of the family. I've called him uncle since I was a child. The nicest and best pilot I know."

"Then you haven't met me yet."

"You fly, too?"

"Helicopters and single-engine airplanes. No seaplanes... yet."

"Not bad!" Now, it was Lilly who was impressed.

Fred helped to stow the clothes, equipment, and provisions in the duo's backpacks. "If I may, I'd like to come with you," he begged. "I can be your Sherpa. We've got Tom, our Wolf Cub. He can manage without me."

Years ago, Lilly's father, Leo Feron, had taken in his sister's straw-haired, autistic son and patiently trained him in the trade. Tom—just four years younger than his cousin, yet in many ways still a child—became wholly absorbed in the skills he had so painstakingly learned. He had difficulties talking to others and understanding facial expressions and body language, and he was overwhelmed by many things. But he looked after the wolves as well as Leo had ever seen, and in return the creatures loved him like no other. It often seemed as though the animals were drawn to Tom because of his gentle nature. He spoke to them in a way beyond words, a gift Lilly could only explain as part of the strange brilliance that sometimes came with his autism. The park staff called him the Wolf Cub, Tom's chosen kin and his family, which is why wolves were called his family.

He preferred to stay inside the timber wolf enclosure, where he had even secretly spent the odd night. The twelve-pack members swarmed around him incessantly, each animal wanting to protect him. There were often fights for the best place at his side. Completely fearless, he would pounce on the quarrelling four-legged friends and join the scuffle. He has never been hurt once.

As shy as he was, Tom lived in Leo Feron's old camper van, a 1983 Ford Econoline Camper. Though still in working order, it has been parked on the quiet side of the building complex for years. Sitting on the footboard of the camper, Lilly regularly shaved the shy boy's fair hair so short that he looked very young and provided him with food, drink, clothes, and anything else he needed. It wasn't much, and he never asked for anything more. The animals and the forest were enough for him.

He roamed the area every day, sometimes appearing here or there like a ghost; no one ever knew where the boy was, but everyone had taken a real liking to him. Tom was the good soul of Feron Wolf Park.

Lilly gripped Fred's shoulders with both hands, and the trainee looked at her with his puppy dog eyes to soften her up.

"Thank you, my redhead, but I need you here," she said urgently. "You know that our Wolf Cub is helpless in many situations. Now, you can show off all that I've taught you. The meat freezer is well stocked. Tom will stay outside to keep an eye on the packs. You can always reach each other via walkie-talkie. You hold down the fort... and keep visitors away, if possible. Stan Hardy will probably show up. Just tell him we're on a wolf safari and'll be back in a few days!"

Fred, though crestfallen, had his spirits improved by the idea of taking on extra responsibility at the farm. "All right, boss. I hope you find some more Beringian wolves. I'll hold down the fort here, look after the house, empty the freezer... You can count on me, Ms. Feron."

"Okay, Freddy. And one more request: We'll reach the lake by mid-morning. Please get this trapper to meet and show us where he saw the wolf. Maybe we can install a few game cameras together and take photos of a whole pack if it exists. Well, wouldn't that be just amazing!"

"You got it, boss. I can imagine him joining in. He's been laying it on pretty thick. This would be his chance to prove it."

"Bingo! You're a great help to me, " she praised him. "And you're also my best intern."

"I'm the only one!"

Fred didn't need to know all the details. Lilly knew that the possible existence of a Neanderthal would only have disturbed him. The matter was highly sensitive, and discretion was advisable.

It was time for Walker to head back to the university. His evening lecture was due to start in twenty minutes. He stepped out into the courtyard, thinking hard. Somewhere, deep inside, he felt there was still something he had to do before the excursion—but what? The vague feeling didn't materialize. He closed his eyes, breathed in the fresh forest air and listened to himself, and suddenly, he felt as if he could hear a songline from his ancestors. The voices of the wandering song described the snow-covered mountains of the Australian Alps, their cold, their ice .... Then, he knew what to do.

The Wrangler's navigation system guided him along the dark forest roads and highways, the quickest route to the university campus. He passed through security without any problems and showed his ID. With his chip card and a scan of his fingerprint, he accessed the Lab for Evolutionary Genetics.

He found what he was looking for in the icebox, wrapped in a double-sterile pack, with the sign "Cindy Klein."

16

Walker's evening lecture on the roots of humanity was more turbulent than expected. The student body was a lively, cheerful bunch of inquisitive would-be adventurers. He took great pleasure in getting them newly excited about the subject that had captivated him for so many years.

Walker's passion for the tribal history of mankind grew from his visit to the rock paintings in Kimberley. As his knowledge of our mysterious ancestors grew, so did his understanding of them. Details about their culture and anatomy made them almost tangible, and he encountered them in many of his dreams.

"You know, long time spans make it difficult for palaeoanthropology because time erases all traces. Well, *almost* all of them. Thanks to new technologies, archaeological finds are now being analyzed much more effectively than just a few decades ago. One example is the excavation of a tiny, sixty-thousand-year-old bone in a cave in the Altai Mountains of Siberia. Not too long ago, an analysis of the genetic material extracted from it revealed that it was the phalanx of a thirteen-year-old girl who was neither a Neanderthal nor an anatomically modern human. She was a Denisova human, who existed in genetic isolation in Asia for several hundred thousand years. The evolutionary development of these hominids was independent.

Neanderthals, Denisovans, and Homo sapiens were very different from each other, but this did not prevent them from producing offspring together about fifty thousand years ago. The result is… you. DNA does not lie. All of us in this room carry genetic material from these three different human forms. Isn't that remarkable?"

Nods of approval flicked around the hall.

"Are these hereditary traits noticeable in any way?" asked a freckled student with striking red curls.

"Oh yes, quite clearly and in many ways. For example, their genes influence our ability to metabolize fat and break down toxins, and they help decide our pigmentation too. Some of us, like you sir, have the light skin and reddish hair of the Neanderthals. And if anyone here is an early riser, that's from them, too. The ability of people in Tibet to adapt to the low-oxygen highlands is also interesting. They owe that to the gene pool of Denisova man, who reached their region one hundred and sixty thousand years ago, long before Homo sapiens."

"Do we know what Neanderthals ate?"

Walker knew that facts that get under the skin make listeners particularly enthusiastic. He contorted his face into a disgusted expression. "I don't think you want to know that much," he said.

Everyone laughed, all the more interested in his answer.

"They were omnivores and ate certain animals, plants, and mushrooms. There was hardly anything left of the roebuck they killed; it was usually completely... *utilized*. There is an analysis of plant residues in Neanderthal tooth enamel. It proves that they preferred to eat the pre-digested stomach contents of the hunted game, presumably to obtain certain nutrients. They may even have liked the aroma. It supposedly has something cheesy about it. Well, maybe it goes well with half-decayed carrion. However, we don't know if they were scavengers. We do know that they loved to barbecue anything that couldn't escape quickly enough."

Such eerily beautiful details enchanted Walker's listeners immensely. His repertoire of fascinating stories and insights was inexhaustible. But today, he focused his lecture on one fundamental truth.

"So, if we call ourselves *human*, who are we? Are we Homo sapiens? No, not exclusively! I want to tell you about a hike that led to the most fateful encounter of mankind.

After Homo sapiens, the anatomically modern human had developed in Africa as an independent species of the genus Homo from Homo erectus. Some of these creatures migrated in groups of hunter-gatherers along the coasts toward Eurasia in several waves of emigration. Seventy thousand years ago, they reached Southeast Asia, Australia, and North Africa, and around fifty thousand years ago, a large Homo sapien population reached present-day Europe.

Momentous encounters took place in Eurasia, where Homo sapiens encountered the different pre-modern human forms: Neanderthals and Denisova man. As fundamentally different as they were, they shared the same habitat. The assumption is that there was hostility between them, but we don't know that. What is certain is that some of them mated with each other.

For hundreds of thousands of years, Neanderthals and Denisovans dominated the Eurasian landscape, even as anatomically modern humans slowly began migrating into the same regions. Until their arrival, they were the undisputed top predators in the food pyramid—skilled hunters, and much smarter than their appearance would suggest.

Our knowledge of them is constantly growing. To describe them as stupid is outdated and inaccurate. Their brains are at least as large as those of modern humans. They had a language; made sophisticated tools from natural materials; hunted as a team; made clothing and jewelry; mastered the complicated production of birch tar as a sort of Stone Age glue; cared for clan members; and probably even believed in an afterlife, given that they buried their dead siblings.

Neanderthals inhabited the Sidrón Cave in northern Spain for thousands of years. Using a mass spectrometer, scientists there recently detected substances in the coating of some excavated teeth that reveal exciting details about their eating habits. Their diet included raw meat and smoked, cooked, and spiced foods. They ate a huge variety of wild plants, including starchy plants such as tubers and wild wheat.

And, since we know that they also had the gene that makes us taste bitter substances, it was particularly revealing to identify components of chamomile and other bitter plants. Chamomile has no nutritional or physiological value; it does not give our body any energy to utilize nutrients. Neanderthals, however, chewed the bitter flower despite its repulsive taste because it has a wonderful healing effect. Our amazing cousins, therefore, knew medicinal plants, used them and passed on their knowledge to others. Isn't that pretty amazing?"

Once again, Walker was delighted to see fascinated students nod approvingly. He took a large sip of tea and readied himself to continue.

"Here's something else just as interesting: compared to us, their robust, muscular bodies required twice as many calories. Despite their enormous strength, they were incredibly sensitive, fleet-footed hunters who were coordinated and strategic when stalking. Together with dozens of clan members, they could take down the largest land mammal of the Pleistocene, the European forest elephant. The elephant bulls reached a shoulder height of over thirteen feet and a live weight of eleven tons, making them almost twice as heavy as the African elephants alive today.

As hunting prey, the colossal proboscideans were unequal opponents. However, the early humans drove them into pits or bogs with excellent coordination. The subsequent dismembering over several days was hard work. Still, it was worth it: a single carcass provided four tons of fresh meat, presumably dried on the fire and preserved."

The redheaded student raised their hand again. "But how can we really know that?"

"Good question! We can't *know* entirely, but it's strongly suggested by charcoal remains near the excavation sites. For weeks, hundreds of clan members fed on a single one of these giants. Neanderthals were hardly the lumbering, sluggish cave dwellers they were still portrayed as in the twentieth century. According to some scientists, they swam, dived, and even mastered seafaring."

Walker paused. The thought of seafaring had been on his mind for years. It is a known fact that several Greek islands were colonized by Neanderthals despite being wholly surrounded by water. And even Flores could only be reached by Homo erectus using a watercraft. Where else could these creatures have gone if they could travel by water?

He concluded his first reading with a thought that had preoccupied him over the past few years and had been a great source of motivation for his research:

"The reasons for and timing of the extinction of our archaic relatives are still not clearly understood. New discoveries are constantly correcting and adding to what we know. Whereas yesterday, early humans were thought to have been extinct for thirty-five thousand years, today, we find evidence that a gene—flow from Denisova man to us—took place around twenty thousand years ago.

What will we find out tomorrow? Well, we're open. Science doesn't hide from new findings; it looks for them because that's what it does!"

At the end of the lecture, Walker was bombarded with questions. The students admired his informal, relaxed manner, and that's exactly how he wanted it. As for the professor himself, he had thoroughly enjoyed his opening lecture. Yet, as he tackled questions from the keen young learners before him, he found that the upcoming expedition was on his mind. Naturally, however, he couldn't talk about it. Discretion was the order of the day.

17

When Lilly reached Great Salt Lake, Uncle Miller was busily undertaking the pre-flight inspection. With meticulous attention, he checked the wings, the propeller, the two floats and water rudders, the fuel quantity, the tank ventilation, and all the lights. Joking that she would never find a man good enough for her, he completed his inspection. To his surprise, and for the first time, she replied that she was no longer sure about that.

Once the expedition equipment had been stowed away, Miller locked the luggage compartment and cleaned the airplane windows. Lilly couldn't stop thinking about the professor, who was still lecturing so late and then using the satnav to guide him to the departure point because he wasn't familiar with the area. She admitted to herself that without him, she hardly would have embarked on this adventure.

Finally, she saw the headlights of the Wrangler approaching. Before dawn, they were seated in the spacious multi-purpose aircraft, a Cessna 208 Caravan Float. Miller took off from Great Salt Lake, after which Utah's capital was named, leaving the water behind and following the course of Veterans Memorial Highway far below. The flight would take around two hours. Due to the clunky floats, it only reached a top speed of around one hundred and eighty miles per hour, but Miller enjoyed this relaxed nature of his life. At his sixtieth birthday party, he had proudly announced to anybody who would listen that the word "rush" had been officially deleted from his vocabulary. For his retirement, he had finally spruced up the interior of his beloved Cessna, installing stretch cover and ambient lighting, flat screens, polished folding tables, and six comfortable leather seats. This gave him a whole new genre clientele. From then on, burnt-out investment bankers and thrill-seeking millionaire widows had flocked to him for their personal adventures. Still, no matter how much money came his way, it was not uncommon for Miller to decide against the lucrative business in favor of a relaxing fishing weekend by the lake.

"Old age is more about the heart," he used to say, "and less about the wallet."

They climbed higher, soon reaching the vast northern national parks, which the veteran pilot knew like the back of his hand. To the east lay Bridger-Teton and Yellowstone, and to the west, Salmon-Challis and Payette unfolded beneath them. Onboard, the mood was exuberant. Miller reminisced and recounted spectacular emergency landings, tricky rescue missions, and one particularly unforgettable experience with his old friend Leo, Lilly's father.

"Your father was almost a wolf himself. That's how well he knew these animals inside and out. He left me in my Cessna in Colville for three freezing cold days and nights because he didn't want to part with an injured she-wolf. She gave birth in the woods and died. When Leo finally showed up at the lake, he had two tiny pups tucked inside his coat. They were still deaf and blind. We took the pups to the wolf park where he raised them with you, Lilly, right?"

"I remember. One of them is still alive. His name is Romulus, and he's a proud seventeen-year-old."

"So, Remus died," Walker concluded.

"Unfortunately. And yes, fine, *well done*, that was the other one's name. You clever professor," she joked.

The seaplane flew over a colorful mountain landscape.

"There they are, the Painted Rocks," Miller called out. "The colors you see down there are made of granite and rhyolite; their shades come from the green, yellow, and orange lichen that covers them."

He used the radio to obtain information about the wind, weather, and traffic. All the while, he flew by sight, effortlessly and unflinchingly as if piloting nothing more than a toy airplane.

"And *there* is Painted Rocks Lake. It's not a lake, but a dam. How's that for knowledge, *professor?*" He teased.

Miller flew in a large circle over the dam, then descended, touched down elegantly on the water, and moved the plane to a jetty. He helped unload the cargo and promised to be ready for the return flight. Lilly hugged him goodbye, thanked him, and kissed him on the cheek. Walker also thanked him warmly.

"Take good care of her," Miller urged him in a serious tone, shaking his hand vigorously.

"Most definitely. Don't worry, sir! I'll be happy to return the favor with a flight over the Outback—if you ever have a few days off."

"Are you also a pilot?"

"Indeed I am. I'd show you with great pleasure." Walker gave him a wink and tipped his hat respectfully.

"Keep the blue side up, Uncle Miller!" Lilly shouted at him.

A horse rider, wearing a beige camouflage outfit, and leading three other horses, approached the jetty.

18

They waved after the blue and white Cessna as it took off and then turned to the trapper, who was tethering the horses to the jetty and filling his water skins. A stocky man in his mid-fifties with a brown moustache had very shaky hands, Lilly noticed he smelled of an unpleasant fusion of whiskey and sweat.

When Fred called him to ask if he was interested in a spontaneous expedition, Stolin promptly agreed. It was his chance for redemption. He had made a fool of himself among his friends with his wolf story, and nobody was buying it. "That was a raccoon, *not* a Beringian wolf," they mocked him. "Or a rabbit. A cutesy little bunny."

Because he was unpopular, bets were already being placed against him, which put him under pressure to back up his fanciful tales. So, Fred's suggestion to work with a wolf expert was very opportune. Her expertise could help him track down the animal and identify it correctly. On top of that, the pelt would be his.

Still, he had no idea that the same wolf had been run almost four hundred miles to the south two days ago, nor did he need to.

"You're lucky!" said Frank Stolin in greeting. "Got the week off." He stared unabashedly at Lilly and gave Walker a blatantly condescending look. It was clear from their first exchange that he intended to shoot the wolf if he saw it again, and nothing these out-of-towners could do would change his mind on that. "You gotta know we already have more than enough of these creatures here," he complained, "and we don't need any that shoulda been eradicated long ago."

His words were as cynical as they were clear, and Lilly knew they would have to be vigilant and discreet with this man. Only he could lead them to where he had encountered the animal, but with this attitude, he posed a danger that had to be countered with caution.

Walker, sensing a tension that needed to be diffused, praised him for his courage and, with a handshake, thanked him for providing the horses. The Australian was not worried about the Beringian wolves, as the chances of encountering another one of these rare animals were slim. If he did, he would do everything he could to thwart the shooting for Lilly's sake alone. Above all, however, it was a matter of tracking down any Neanderthals that might be hunting in the area.

Lilly was equally aware of this. Nevertheless, she explained to the trapper that it would be better for his reputation to show the public pictures of a live Beringian wolf rather than a dead one.

"You're a smart man, Mr. Stolin," she said coolly. "Don't get your hands dirty! Be the outdoorsman who protects rare species. You're sure to be praised when you discover this prehistoric animal. It's guaranteed to cause a sensation among your friends and in the press. Y'know, National Geographic give you a nice payday for an article like this."

"Ms. Feron is right," Walker agreed. "You'll go down in Montana history as a true hero."

Stolin had to admit that he liked this version at least as much as the shooting version. He would think about it, he said with feigned uncertainty, and recounted what had happened during his infamous sighting of the Beringian wolf:

"That beast was just lucky," he announced bitterly. "I wanted to shoot him, but somethin' stopped me. I won't forget it."

"What happened?"

"So, I'm on my horse, ridin' through the damn countryside, and suddenly, he appears in front of me. I know gray wolves, I'd like to think, and

I've killed a few in my time. But this one's different. It looks like one o' them beasts on display at the Beringia Museum. I immediately take aim at it. But just before the shot, I hear a thump, and my stupid horse rises as if he'd been bitten by a tarantula. Naw, I still don't know what the hell it was. His front legs go up. The bastard almost throws me off. Normally, he stays calm, even when a big grizzly appears."

"What was it? What made your horse so wild?"

"Haven't got a clue, miss. I jus' had a real bad feeling. Like we weren't alone. You know? Like there was someone else there, watchin'."

Lilly and Walker flashed each other a cursory nod.

"Well, when my horse finally calmed down, the wolf had already disappeared. As I said, he was lucky. He got away again!"

The three of them set about tying up their equipment on the pack-horse. Stolin then spread out a large map on the dusty ground and marked with a red pencil an area about thirty miles to the northwest. It was in the Selway–Bitterroot Wilderness mountains, one of the largest designated wilderness areas in the United States. Stolin moved closer to the map, scanned it and finally pressed a small cross into the paper with his long, dirty fingernail.

"I think that's where it was," he said. "Can set off right away. Hope you're not beginners when it comes to ridin'. We'll probably spend two or three days in the saddle and not meet a soul. You know, there are still a few campsites by this lake, sites for motorhomes, a boat ramp, and a landing stage. That sorta thing. But up there is just the wretched wilderness. Many thousands of square miles of nothing but damned forests and mountains. It can kill ya. There are moose, white-tailed deer and bighorn sheep. And, of course, bears, coyotes and wolves. Tell me right away if you're no good on horseback. A bitta humility might jus' save your life."

Walker had already swung himself onto the piebald Mustang in one leap, casually adjusted his Akubra and skillfully guided the horse once around in a circle on the spot. *There's your proof,* he thought. He then patted his horse gently on the neck and whispered something in the language of his Australian ancestors.

Lilly mounted, clicked her tongue, and steered her light brown mare to the narrow wooden landing stage. The horse jumped onto it in one leap, trotted to the end, performed a pirouette, and galloped back to the men.

"She's sure-footed and beautiful," she enthused, "a Morgan mare, isn't she?"

"Yup, you're right. Let's go then," shouted Stolin, visibly pleased with the successful demonstration, if not a little disappointed he hadn't been able to show one of them up.

Two hours later, the three riders were surrounded by fragrant pine forests, rugged cliffs, and picturesque gorges. They spotted peregrine falcons in the bright blue sky above the overwhelmingly beautiful mountain landscape. Three hundred feet ahead of them, a mighty elk trotted calmly into the woods, and at a mountain lake full of trout, great blue herons and bald eagles went fishing.

They took their first break at midday. Walker looked after the horses while Lilly borrowed Stolin's topographical map and unfolded it on the ground. Meanwhile, the trapper searched for damaged cartridges in his case and checked his hunting rifle. He ensured that the rifle's bolt had play and the rifle barrel was accurate. The trapper raved about his bolt-action rifle as if it were his own flesh and blood. He knew the technical details inside out.

Stolin prized his Ruger American Rifle Predator. Its long, precise barrel and rail-mounted scope made it perfect for picking off trophies from a safe distance, and though it sometimes jammed, he kept it clean and treated it with care. Over time, the rifle became more than a tool; he slept beside it, kissed its steel like a lover. Even the ammunition felt special to him—light .223 Remington cartridges with low recoil, treasures he carried in abundance on every hunt.

He was particularly impressed by a description from a gun dealer. It said: "The cartridge's polymer tip and the cavity underneath ensure high precision and a controlled, even expansion in the game's body." In his opinion, this was almost poetically formulated and perfectly accurate. The bullet holes appeared extremely even, a fact that regularly made him proud. It would be no different in the body of the endangered Beringian wolf. It was a sight he was already relishing.

Lilly noticed right away that Stolin's topographical map didn't reveal much. She knew about maps; her father had familiarized her with his collection before his death. This map, though, lacked any real detail and seemed largely unreliable. The trapper, she realized, was using an inaccurate, digitally produced map. As is so often the case with modern maps, it was almost impossible to recognize the features of the landscape clearly.

To make matters worse, the graphic editors had converted the given data without sufficient local geographical knowledge. Comparing the details was hardly possible in vast, deserted areas like this one. She sighed, knowing that—even if this map was of very little help— it was their only hope of not ending up lost in the wilderness.

While Stolin was stowing the rifle and accessories, Walker came over from the horses and showed Lilly a picture on his smartphone. It was a sharp photo of the mysterious engraving on the flattened side of the bone head. Walker had taken it in his kitchenette and enhanced the contrast with a digital filter.

"Doesn't this look like a miniature map?" he asked her. He placed the cell phone on the large map. "Maybe a certain place is significant to our distant cousin."

"You mean some kind of geographical symbolism?" asked Lilly.

"Possibly."

"So, let's assume this is a miniature map, and the spearman was hunting the Beringian wolf in these mountains..."

"... then, there could theoretically be a match between the two images somewhere," Walker finished her sentence. "If that's the case, we would have to find the configuration of the engraved symbols somewhere on this Bitterroot map."

"Stolin's map sucks," Lilly said disappointedly. "It just shows the terrain by contour lines and a few other structures. You can only guess if this is a peak, a mountain saddle, a lake or a river course. We can't be sure because there are no clear landmarks and basically no details to speak of."

Walker nodded. "I noticed. No roads, towns, waterways or power lines in this wilderness. So, we have to make do with what little we have."

They were startled to see Frank Stolin standing right behind them.

"What's wrong?" he asked provocatively. "I don't have a better map, if that's ya problem. At least the scale is pretty darn big: one to fifty thousand. Go on, open it completely!"

The Australian helped Lilly spread the paper and placed a stone on each corner.

Stolin became suspicious: "What kinda thing is that on your phone?"

He had seen it. Walker had to let him in on it, but he only revealed half the truth: "It's from my cousin. He met the Beringian wolf, too. We're wondering if it's a miniature map."

Stolin's gaze darkened. "Your cousin? Listen, this isn't a scavenger hunt! What's your cousin doing in this wasteland? Is he playing a game with us? Listen carefully! I'm not going to be made a fool of, understood? I wanna track down the beast. Is that clear?"

Lilly managed to de-escalate things. "Don't worry, Mr. Stolin."

Walker knelt close to her, turned his phone around, enlarged the photo and pointed to individual symbols in the engraving. "Let's assume," he said, "that these signs show the way. At the top, the artist has engraved three beautiful, round pinecones. A winding line leads from them to this misshapen spot."

"The line could be a stream, and the spot could be a rock," added Lilly. "And the big border next to it... a forest? Take a look. It shows a little stick figure with a head, arms, and legs."

"The human symbol could be a dwelling."

"Nonsense!" said Stolin disparagingly. "No two mountains here are the same. There are all kinds of lakes and streams. Mountains, valleys, cliffs, plateaus, natural paths, meadows, and forests exist in thousands of combinations. Remember who *lives* out here. You can't know everythin' from books."

What the trapper didn't realize was that if there were many variations and no two shapes were alike, there was a real possibility of finding a clear match. If the engraving was a map, it was like a fingerprint with a counterpart somewhere out there, waiting to be found. And that was an opportunity. All they had to do was find the match on Stolin's topographical map.

They continued to search for similarities, concentrating on the region around Boulder Peak in the direction they were moving. Some lakes were similarly shaped, but the other images did not match the original. Stolin looked increasingly glum. The image of the bullet wound in the wolf's neck was increasingly fading.

Lilly suddenly nudged Walker and pointed to one of the winding mountain formations. "That height limit on the map..." she said excitedly, "... isn't it the same shape as what I called a forest?"

Looking at the map, then the mountain, Walker concluded that both outlines seemed almost identical. The difference in height decreased rapidly toward the inside. And that was not all. Walker turned and moved his phone until the two images were exactly next to each other.

"The rest seems to fit as well," he confirmed. "So, it's a valley, a deep gorge in the middle of the mountains. And the supposed rock on the engraving could actually be a lake. In any case, the shapes match exactly."

Lilly tried not to sound too euphoric. "According to the scale, the lake should be around three-thirty by three-thirty feet. And apparently, a mountain stream flows into it."

"Whether stream or path, the course is always parallel to this contour line."

Everything clicked. That couldn't be a coincidence. Frank Stolin also recognized the similarities. He stared at the map absent-mindedly. A hint of fear flitted across his unkempt visage.

"No, no, no!" he cried timidly. "Wild horses couldn't drag me there."

"Why is that?" Walker wanted to know.

"I'm telling you, the area is dangerous. We trappers avoid it like hell. The mountains are steep, treacherous... completely inaccessible. We even have a name for this area: the Bermuda Mountains."

"Bermuda Mountains? Like the Bermuda Triangle?"

"Right. Tons of people have gone missing there. Steep rock faces, dense forests, impassable obstacles, no possibility of landing, not even for helicopters. From above, from the air, everything looks densely wooded and rocky. But you don't want to go into it on foot. You're never gonna find your way out."

"But that's *exactly* where we have to go!" shouted Walker and Lilly in near unison. Together, they refolded the map and returned it to the trapper.

Fear was written blatantly over Stolin's face. "We're already at an altitude of four thousand feet," he said in a broken voice. "The weather could be a problem up there."

Lilly strode energetically toward him. "We'll manage just fine without you, Mr. Stolin," she said confidently. "Don't you worry about us!"

Stolin thought hard and then said meekly, "All right, I'll come with you, but this is on you."

They quickly got ready and saddled up. At midday, the summer sky was still cloudless, but the air was already much colder. They rode higher and higher up toward Boulder Peak. The Bermuda Mountains lie behind another mountain range, around twelve miles away. Frank Stolin advised trekking around the western slope a few hundred feet below the summit and descending in a northerly direction. They succeeded, although the descent proved to be risky and arduous. Now and then, there were rockfalls, and the riders often had to walk and lead the horses by the halter. With every step downhill, it became much warmer again.

In the afternoon, the group reached Boulder Creek, a beautiful-wooded valley unchanged over thousands of years, through which crystal-clear water carves its way. The horses grazed on the banks. Stolin lit a campfire. Walker used a net to catch a large mountain whitefish, which he gutted, speared, grilled, and sprinkled with sea salt. Nearby, Lilly picked wild blueberries and bright red lobster mushrooms, which were not bad when roasted. She and Walker agreed they tasted like seafood. The berries were for dessert. Stolin cleaned his rifle, got well drunk on Old Crow, and soon fell asleep.

Deeply moved by the unadulterated charm of this unique landscape, Lilly and Walker strolled along the river for a while. Nowhere, they agreed, was it more peaceful and carefree than here. They knew they shared a passion for the animal and plant world, for the origins of mankind, and also for science, but there was more: a kindred spirit. With and without words, they understood each other, felt what was felt by the other, and sensed a wonderful attraction.

A little less than two hundred feet in front of them, four young foxes were rolling in the evening sun.

"Come on, *quietly*."

Lilly and Walker could get within a few steps without the animals noticing them. It was only at the last moment that three foxes bolted, disappearing in an amber blur. The fourth young fox saw no chance of escaping, so instead of jumping away, he put one paw in front of the other with strange, jerky movements.

"Look, he's stealing away with a break dance," Walker whispered. "Why is he doing that?"

"Camouflage! I assume it's for camouflage. Chameleons and praying mantises do the same."

"You're right! When they approach the prey, they bob and do a little dance. That seems to confuse others."

They moved away from the young fox so as not to frighten him. As they walked, Walker spun around and imitated Michael Jackson's famous moonwalk.

Lilly laughed in her delightful way, "Oh no, please don't confuse me too!"

In the distance, as smoke from the campfire rose gray and silent, the evening concert of the forest birds began to mingle with the delicate murmur of the creek. For Lilly, perfect happiness in life seemed to be in this very place, and at this very moment, she realized that the man next to her was an essential part of it.

Walker, who felt the same, took hold of her shoulders, pulled her gently toward him and whispered to her: "You and I in paradise."

"Me and you in paradise," Lilly replied and snuggled up close.

19

Another day has passed. Twilight settles heavily on the shady forest until all shadows are lost. Unnoticed, the hunter sneaks up to the trapped wolves near the bobos' dwellings. The lights of the high heads shine like many tiny fires in the darkness. He remains part of the shadows—black as birch tar, invisible and silent. He has come to take what is his.

He comes close to the captive wolves, surrounded by a shiny net. It has an opening like a fish trap, but it is closed. He marvels at the hard material of the net. When the animals scent him, he senses their fear and awe of him, the lord of the forest and the mountains. Submission gleams in their shining eyes. He controls them without words and tells them to be quiet and obey. Under the cover of night, he leaves them and approaches the wondrous buildings of the bobos. It is also dead silent there. He circles them as silently as a mountain lion.

Old Watka told me about the high-headed people enough to make me avoid them. Their way of life makes no sense. They violate the wilderness, fill their existence with useless things, destroy the habitat of plants and animals, burn the forest and poison the water, create substances that do not decompose and throw them into the plant kingdom. They fight among themselves because they believe it benefits them; they want to grow and change everything all the time. Why change what is good?

An unexpectedly bright light shines from one of the buildings, momentarily blinding Omu. He closes his eyes. When he opens them again, he recognizes movement inside. He sees a big bobo running from one room to another and recognizes him: the red-haired man who carried off the wolf. Now, he is the guardian of the carcass.

The dwelling is as dense as a marmot's burrow, but Omu has to get in. Now, the wolves in the enclosure howl because a vehicle is approaching. Its lights cut through the darkness, and Omu takes cover.

A gaunt man gets out of the car. The redhead opens the door and lets him into his dwelling.

20

Like everything else about this exciting event, Stan Hardy's surprise evening visit was highly interesting for Fred. The intern proudly showed the ranger around the premises of the wolf park facility, of which he was now the temporary chief administrator, and asked him lots of questions about Uinta–Wasatch National Park, where Stan worked.

As a spooky crowning touch to the tour, he showed him the Beringian wolf laid out in the small cold room and told him about Stolin's amazing sighting of the animal east of Salmon River.

It's a hell of a long way away, Stan thought as he meticulously brushed the dust off his ranger pants.

Over a hot coffee, Stan asked when Lilly would be back. When he learned she had decided to go on an impromptu expedition with the professor, he asked: "Why so spur-of-the-moment? It's all a bit ominous... just like that crazy thing she discovered."

"What crazy thing?"

Stan told them about the mysterious archaic spearhead, and soon both of them were putting two and two together. Fred remembered what his boss had said about the unusually long distance the Beringian wolf had traveled, that something could have propelled the wolf over that distance.

"What could that be?"

"Well, now." Stan deduced. "It's conceivable that his hunter is pursuing him. He wants to get this particular weapon back."

"Tracked *this* far?"

Fred felt a chill run down his spine as he looked through the wide panoramic window. Outside, it was almost pitch black. Only a few small LEDs surrounded the wide courtyard.

"Then, it must be a damn capable hunter," he said.

"You're right," Stan said, thinking of Jack Manchin's words. "Maybe it's a Native American. You know, First Nations people. Some of them don't want to live in the cities. Some still use traditional hunting weapons to preserve their culture."

Fred was still staring into the darkness when he noticed the enclosure wolves were behaving unusually. They didn't seem to want to calm down after Stan's arrival. The visitor had been in the house for almost half an hour, but the growling and howling hadn't ceased.

Vocalizations are a part of every wolf park. At dusk, the howling can be heard for several miles. In addition to sophisticated acoustic language, wolves communicate using body language, facial expressions, scents, and touch. Lilly has been familiar with this since childhood and is a master at interpreting and using this complex communication. Working within the wolf enclosures would be impossible and dangerous without this knowledge. Fred, however, knew that he still had much to learn before being granted full access to the packs.

The unrelenting nervousness of the wolves that evening was undoubtedly unusual. He ran from the kitchen to the office, Lilly's large work and living area. Stan followed him. The surveillance system monitor was installed on one wall.

"The wolves are upset," Fred muttered as he looked at a monitor. "Normally, they relax as soon as the visitor enters the house."

Three of the four fenced areas were each equipped with two surveillance cameras with night vision capability. The largest separate cell, where the dozen timber wolves formed a pack, had four cameras.

Fred watched the live feed as three animals in the large enclosure put their heads down and howled; others trotted excitedly up and down the fence, and some crouched quietly, staring in the direction of the buildings where Fred and Stan were located. *Have they spotted something?*

"They're not howling at the moon, right?" said Stan.

"The moon thing is a myth anyway."

"One is even barking I thought wolves didn't bark."

"Myth number two. They do... sometimes." Stan stood close to the monitor.

"Why don't you show me what it looked like an hour ago?"

"Okay, I can do that."

Fred went back sixty minutes in the recording. The wolves were scattered around the area, sleeping or dozing.

"If I'm not mistaken," said Stan, "I hadn't arrived at that time. They were very quiet then."

Fred clicked forward on the recording, minute by minute, until two of the animals stood up, pricked their ears, and looked intently in one specific direction. In the minutes that followed, the pack gathered, one by one, around the lead wolf, a mighty black and gray male almost six and a half feet long.

"That big guy in the middle is called Spirit," said Fred. "He has these piercing yellow eyes that hypnotize you. Hence the name."

The recording continued. Instead of adhering to their hierarchy, the animals moved closer together. They raised their hackles, and some tucked in their tails and flattened their ears. They looked intimidated.

"What's happening?" Stan asked. "Which way are they looking?"
"Wait!"

Fred clicked and switched to another camera with an offset angle. He was startled.

"There!"

Like a ghost, a stocky, athletic figure stood close to the fence. Fred could not place the silhouette. It couldn't be Lilly's cousin Tom, the Wolf Cub. He was much slimmer. This figure seemed to be staring so intently that the enclosed wolves became utterly, unfamiliarly submissive.

"Who's that?" Fred blurted out.

Stan whispered, "I guess... that's the guy."

"The pursuer? The Indian? Or whatever?"

"The hunter. He's looking for the wolf. He wants to get him." Uneasiness crept into the pit of Fred's stomach. He began to sweat.

"Damn! Damn! What do we do now? Do you have a gun?"

"In the car."

"No, don't go out," Fred implored him. "You'd better stay in the house!"

"Do you have one here? Is there a gun in the building? Or another kinda weapon? Anything!"

"I think so... probably. But where?" Fred thought hard, rubbing his temples. "Wait, I'll look for it." He disappeared into one of the storerooms.

Stan nervously tucked his shirt into his pants, looked around the room, and feverishly thought about what he should do now. He dimmed the lights in the living room area because he couldn't think of anything better to do. It's safer in the dark, he thought. Then, he felt his way through various rooms and checked the windows and doors.

One bathroom window was unlocked. He locked it and paused, listening as if paralyzed. He heard his heart pounding, Fred rummaging around in one of the back rooms. And then he heard something else. A growl? Was it coming from outside? Or was it from inside the house?

Where is Fred?

As if surrounded by thick mud, he stomped from the bathroom into the hallway. The smell of animal sweat filled the corridor, triggering nausea in him. At the end of the corridor, the steel door of the small cold room where the Beringian wolf was laid out gleamed.

He noticed that the door was not completely closed; it was ajar. Frosty air was seeping out. *The trainee definitely closed it earlier—I watched him do it!*

His breath caught in his throat. He concentrated on the subtlest noises, fear preventing him from taking another step. There was the low hum of the air conditioning, and something else echoed from the small room in front of him: a strange snorting, rattling breath like that of an animal, perhaps a bear, then a dull crash, as if bones were shattering.

He wanted to run away but couldn't. He stood, rooted to the spot, staring at the steel door. The cold air seeped out and flowed around his feet, turning his toes to ice until they ached.

Where on earth is Fred?

21

The ice wolf lies cold and stiff in front of the hunter. He has finally reached him. He and the wolf have made it this far; both have reached their destination.

Omu grabs the animal's head with his left hand and its shoulder with his right. Like the claws of a golden eagle, his fingers grip relentlessly, digging deep into the lifeless flesh. Then, Omu tenses his muscles, twisting the dead animal's spine with his arms as if it were a rotten piece of wood. He stretches the wolf's neck forward and presses the head down to the chest until he breaks open the animal's neck with a violent jerk.

The hunter stares at the open, empty wound in the middle of the furless patch. As if struck by lightning, he realizes the engraved spearhead is no longer lodged in place. It has gone.

22

"Uuaahhrr!"

A bloodcurdling primal scream from inside the cold room tore through the air and drove into Stan Hardy's stiff limbs. The steel door burst open with a mighty thud, and Omu stood before him. At once, the ranger felt as if he had been cast in concrete and could only stare straight ahead at him.

Resentment and displeasure distorted the Neanderthal's bulging face, with its thick brow ridges and broad fleshy nose. His reddish hair was short and shaggy. Clumps of fine, rust-colored whiskers sprouted from the skin, tanned by the sun, weathered by it and the wind, and crisscrossed by deep furrows.

Stan was particularly disturbed by the strong-willed, intelligent human gaze from Omu's deep, shadowy eye sockets, which did not match the strangely primitive shape of his skull. It was a gaze that seemed to penetrate him effortlessly.

He had nothing to counter this muscular bundle of strength and aggression. His opponent suddenly overpowered him without any effort, hitting into Stan like a thunderbolt. His knees buckling, the ranger realized that Fred was standing right behind him. He heard a shot, and then his eyes went black. His spindly legs gave way.

23

The blackout only lasted a few seconds, but he still found it difficult to regain full consciousness.

Someone shook him and shouted: "Stan... Mr. Hardy... wake up already! Quick, I need help here!"

A bright neon lamp on the ceiling almost blinded him, and for a moment he thought he was in a hospital recovery room. Then reality set in: he was lying on the cold, hard floor. The room was narrow and long. He must have fallen and hit his head. Ice-cold air was flowing toward him down the corridor. And there was something else, something that was preoccupying him emotionally, paralyzing him with fear. Something terrifying.

Again, he heard the pleading voice, distorted slightly in his ringing ears: "Stan, please. He's too heavy. We have to drag him to the office."

Gradually, an image of reality was emerging. He was not in a hospital or home but in the wolf park. With great effort, he propped himself up on his elbows and looked down the corridor. Now, he saw it: right in front of him rested the horrible, misshapen creature with its abnormally bulging head and the reddish-haired body of a weightlifter. It lay limp and motionless like hunted game, which did little to reassure him. Clad in leather and fur, it clutched a pouch, while a strange axe and equally obscure knife lay next to it. A purple tongue hung limply from its large mouth. Fred was tugging fiercely at the creature's arm, almost panicking, without moving it as much as an inch.

Now, he realized that Fred was struggling in vain. The trainee was frantic and red with exertion.

Stan pushed himself upright against the pull of gravity; his skull roared, and he staggered on unsteady legs. "Wait, let me help you."

"Into the office with him—that big room back there!" panted Fred. "Come on, come on, there's a crate!"

"Isn't he dead?"

"No, just tasered. I tasered him. I was right behind you when you fainted. You hit the ground like a sack of potatoes. I had a clear shot, I fired and it hit him. He wasn't expecting that. Come on, quickly! He could wake up at any moment! What is this thing anyway?"

Stan saw the stun gun lying on the floor and two insulated wires leading to the stunned savage. One of the two projectiles was lodged in his chest, the second in his cheek. He asked no further questions, grabbed the other arm, and pulled.

Together, they dragged the leaden body with small backward steps, complete with the taser wires, through the narrow corridor into the office, across the white-tiled floor of the treatment area, past the operating table and couch to the alcove where the stainless steel wolf crate stood. Once there, Fred crawled in through the hatch, panting and sweating, and dragged the body inside with all his might while Stan lifted and pushed as best he could from the outside. There was a heavy clatter as Omu's skull banged against the metal frame.

"His head is heavier than a cannonball."

Gradually, they heaved him into the cage. One more tug, and they did it. Exhausted, the trainee leaned against the bars to catch his breath.

"Now come out of there!" Stan urged him. "Come, come!"

Fred's horn-rimmed glasses were steaming up. He looked for the cloth in his jeans pockets but couldn't find it. So, he used his sweatshirt.

"What are you doing? Come on! Come on!"

Fred continued cleaning. With his glasses back on his nose, he finally began to climb over the stinking, motionless body and out into the open... when the creature began to stir.

Omu had awoken!

The being gasped in pain, rattled and turned around stolidly. Fred shrank back and pressed himself into the corner of the crate. It was impossible to get past him. Now, he was trapped, together with the monster.

Omu straightened up, sluggish and dazed. He noticed the redhead next to him but was initially more interested in the strangely shiny object they were in. Then he noticed the wires still embedded in his skin and remembered that the redhead had fired them at him. Outraged, he grabbed Fred's foot, abruptly pulled it towards him like a branch, grabbed him by the collar, pointed at the projectile in his chest and made strange noises.

Fred was scared to death. "No, please don't!" he pleaded, knowing he couldn't escape his fate. Unable to form a clear thought, he only noticed Omu's pungent body odor and blathered: "I'm screwed!"

But now it was Stan Hardy who pulled the trigger. Thanks to some quick thinking, he grabbed the stun gun and fired a second time. He didn't have to aim, as the wires were still in the skin. Once again, the electrical impulses instantly immobilized Omu. His body crashed to the grid floor, twitching.

"Get in!" Fred shouted enthusiastically as if he had scored a goal in the World Cup final; he quickly removed the barbed projectiles from Omu's body and forced his way out through the crate's hatch. He promptly threw in three bottles of water and padlocked the steel door. "What madness!"

Stun gun in hand, Stan sat languidly on a folding chair and stared, Bewildered, at the stainless steel cage. "I owed you that," he said, exhausted. "You saved my life!"

"What do we do now?"

"We recover. And we wait for my boss. Under *no* circumstances are we calling the police. This is a case for science, not for the state, much less the press. Let Ms. Feron decide what to do with him. The world has never seen anything like it. This is not a *normal* burglar; this is something quite peculiar!"

"Caught like a predator, you could almost feel sorry for him. Well, he's not exactly a lap dog either."

Fred fetched a six-pack of Templin Lager from the fridge and moved a second folding chair next to the ranger's chair. The beer flowed coolly down his throat. They reflected on what had happened, and soon Fred was freely recounting stories of his most embarrassing misadventures. The unlocked safety pin he swallowed as an infant; the swimming pool he nearly drowned in after he gorged himself on rum fruit as a toddler; and the large-scale search after he got lost in the woods on a Boy Scouts night hike. He considered himself lucky to have had his only asthma attack during his job interview with UFA, Utah's largest fire department, another mishap, but one that ultimately led him to a better place.

'FEARLESS KEEPER WANTED!' he read in the *Salt Lake Tribune* the following day. That's how he came to Feron Wolf Park.

"It was a good find, all right. A real stroke of luck. Lilly made me feel safe and accepted as part of the family here. She takes me as I am, accepts my weaknesses, and builds on my strengths; she stands by me, which feels pretty good."

"One of those strengths, Fred, is certainly the gift of the gab," Stan replied and clinked glasses with him.

In the middle of the night, they sat in front of a wolf crate like the audience of a play in which a monster would awaken at any time.

Dutifully, Stan called Margaret and told her that he was on a night assignment and that she needn't worry. He added that he would tell her everything later, but wasn't truly sure he'd know where to begin. Exhausted, he leaned back and took another sip of beer. His head was pounding. The shock was deep in his bones, yet the beer helped him regain a little stability and confidence.

To avoid being embarrassed because of his outward appearance, Stan had spent his life trying to remain inconspicuous, keeping to himself emotionally and not letting anything get to him. Provocative gestures, phrases, and looks usually rolled off him like water off a duck's back. All that, however, was quashed in this encounter. Effortlessly, the creature had penetrated his protective shell, looked through him, and brutally exposed his true inner self. Then, he fell to the ground as if his brain had been reprogrammed.

He was exhausted now, but he felt surprisingly well and, gradually, realized why. Yes, he, looked weird, but didn't that make him as unique as this creature? Nothing seemed wrong with that; on the contrary, Stan felt authentic, and that gave him an inner strength, a new self-confidence.

At his feet was the stainless steel cage containing the creature they had overpowered together. Perfect teamwork, not bad at all! He pulled out his small, fine clothes brush, which was more than just an ordinary cleaning utensil for him. The bristly thing made it possible to feel surfaces without touching them directly. In addition, the back of the brush was shiny and slightly curved. He looked surprisingly normal when he looked at his distorted reflection in the varnish.

It all depends on perspective, he told himself. *We all have our own unique appearance—the more unique, the better. You are who you are. Own it and be brave!*

There it lay, quietly snoring, about to regain consciousness. Stan couldn't help but feel sorry for the creature.

"A burglar imprisoned in a crate for wolves," he muttered. "Isn't it inhumane to crate him like that?"

Fred lolled next to him in the deckchair. "Just look at him! He's no ordinary intruder. Tell me, is this an ordinary intruder? What do you think?"

"Not at all! What if he breaks out?"

"Nah, nah, he can't get out there. How could he? We'll wait for Ms. Feron. Hopefully, she and that Australian will be back soon before any snoopers show up. We don't need any hype right now."

Stan thought about it, rubbing his long, unshaven chin thoughtfully. *What is it that makes that man so strange? Where did he come from?* There was nothing like him. No category seemed to fit, no matter how long he searched. No Inuit, no Amazonian Indian, no native of Polynesia, no Aborigine, no Mongolian—nothing was like him. He was an anomaly. To dismiss him as a crazy, drunken vagrant or a disabled person lost in the woods seemed equally unrealistic. His worn clothing was made with skill from leather and other natural materials. Nothing about him was modern or normal.

Finally, thinking of Professor Walker, he came up with another category into which the primal creature might fit. As soon as the thought arose, however, he fought to suppress it.

In any case, what was certain was that it weighed a ton and was a phenomenal and possibly dangerous being.

"A Neanderthal!" Fred declared as if there could be nothing more normal, rewarding himself with a large gulp of lager. "A real Neanderthal!"

The trainee knew too little to fully appreciate the implications of this realization. What was more important to him was what he and Stan had achieved. He dared himself to envision the applause of his boss when she returned to see his work. After all, this was looking like a perfect performance; the intruder had been arrested, and the danger averted. His animal body odor still clung to Fred's clothes: sour, masculine, extraordinary. The Neanderthal was about to wake up, and things would surely get intense in the cage. Yet Ms. Feron had always said that you could rely on a stainless steel cage of this design, and he trusted her judgment tremendously.

As another satisfied sip of beer trickled down his throat, however, the curtain went up, and the performance began. The prisoner woke up from his stupor, rolled slowly onto his back, and groaned in pain. His breathing was rumbling and heavy, barely conscious at first. Gradually, though, he became aware of his situation, struggled to his feet, straightened up as much as possible, crawled in circles as if locked in a daze, and finally crouched down in the far corner of his inescapable trap.

Stan and Fred didn't move. Contrary to all their expectations, the Neanderthal remained calm: no tantrums, panic, or aggression. He stayed calmly crouched, observing the shiny bars around him, peering out to examine the strange room, the office.

Omu lightly pressed his foot against the padlocked steel door and eyed the strangers sitting there staring at him, mesmerized and haughty. He noticed the transparent water bottles beside him. They were just lying there; the water was visible, but it wasn't running out of them. *How strange these high-headed people are!*

"He's thirsty, Fred. Why don't you show him how to open a bottle," said Stan, caught slightly off-guard by his own feeling of care toward their captive.

With a firm nod, Fred dutifully got up, fetched a bottle from the fridge, and moved closer to the crate.

"Look here," he said to Omu, unscrewing the bottle demonstratively and taking a sip, "That's how you do it!"

Omu looked on wearily, sighed and signaled disinterest. He made a pitiful impression, and that's what he wanted. *I'll get you one day!*

Stan also came closer to the crate. "Is he too stupid not to open and drink from it?"

"Or too *smart*. I think he's too smart, Stan. Look at his skull. You can fit more brains in there than in mine and yours put together!"

"That's true enough. Do you think he is hungry?"

"Well, his bag is back there; let's see what's inside."

Fred shook the contents of the bag onto the floor. In addition to stones and peculiar objects made of other natural materials, a smaller sack of soft, smooth leather dropped at Fred's feet, skillfully tied with a raffia cord. He opened it, unfolded it, and found a large piece of raw meat. It smelled fresh and was covered in a bed of green herbs.

"Oh, man! That doesn't look like something from McDonald's."

"Just give it to him. Let's see what he does with it," said Stan. "But… be careful!"

The trainee paused, gauging how to keep his distance. He knew the trick—he'd done it countless times at the park, pitching meat to the wolves from behind the bars. In one of the smaller enclosures, eight polar wolves lived in a raw, uneasy hierarchy, wild and untouched by human hands. From the ramp above he would cast down whole haunches of venison, watching the pack surge and snarl as the offering hit the ground.

The twelve hand-tamed timber wolves were housed in the neighboring enclosure, including five pups from a year earlier. Due to their close bond, Lilly and Tom often fed them from their hands. Tom, the Wolf Cub, even wrestled and played with them on occasion. Over several months, Lilly had slowly introduced Fred to the pack until, with time, he too was able to enter the area— albeit accompanied by her—to check the fences and maintain the enclosure. He brought the meals in with a wheelbarrow and delivered them to the wolves.

While the boss was away, however, he and Tom were categorically forbidden from opening the entrances to this area—a fact Lilly had made clear with one of her trademark assertive expressions. They threw the meat over the fence for the polar wolves, which was the safest method. Lilly insisted on following this rule because she was responsible. Something could always happen. If a keeper stumbled in the enclosure and injured himself, the pack would likely see him as prey and attack.

Regarding trust and taming, there is a significant difference between wolves and domestic dogs, which Lilly once made very clear to Fred: "Unlike domestic dogs," she explained, "wolves are fearful and unpredictable throughout their lives. They can never be tamed completely, even if hand-reared. You see, wolf pups explore their environment two weeks earlier than dog pups, at a time when they only have their sense of smell. Because they can't see or hear, they do not become accustomed to acoustic and visual impressions. By the time their eyes and ears open, the socialization phase is already complete. Strange noises and objects now appear threatening. On the other hand, dogs cannot only smell but also hear and see when they first set out to explore. This allows them to make friends with people, birds, horses and even cats at an early age."

The Stone Age man must have been starving. Fred and Stan agreed as much, but they had few ideas about how to feed him. Hand feeding was out of the question. After some back and forth, Fred decided to throw in the food.

"Okay, I'm going to play a game of toss," he said arrogantly, winking at Stan and fastening Omu's food bag as best he could.

As he sat motionless in his corner, the Neanderthal's small, alert brown eyes followed the redhead's every move. Fred moved his throwing arm, took aim, and skillfully lobbed the round leather bag up onto the middle of the crate with a slight backward spin. It landed on the steel grid but was too big to fall through.

"Great throw. It's in a good spot," laughed Stan.

Still, Omu didn't touch his food over. *Come on... I dare you!*

"What a bummer! Okay, wait!" Fred ran around the crate to the side opposite Omu. "Stay where you are," he called to him warningly, still uncertain as to whether he understood him at all.

As Omu remained still, Fred dared to make a quick advance, bent far over the cage and tried to knock the bag of food in with one blow of his fist. He succeeded, but hadn't reckoned with the Neanderthal's speed; he catapulted himself like a spring and grabbed Fred's wrist with an iron grip. Fred screamed like a banshee, as did Stan, who didn't know how to help. Grinning fiercely, Omu pulled Fred's arm toward him with enormous force.

However, the horror did not last long. Omu abruptly let go of the arm and released Fred. A bizarre, animalistic laugh resounded from his mouth, and then he casually unscrewed the bottle as if he had practiced it dozens of times and rewarded his successful performance with a large gulp of mineral water.

25

After a quick breakfast before sunrise, Lilly, Walker, and Stolin packed up their horses and began their second ascent into the next mountain range of the desolate Bitterroot wilderness.

Lilly was wholly absorbed in the setting. She felt that her father, from whom she had learned so much about flora, fauna and fungi on countless hikes, was particularly close to her here. It almost seemed as if he was riding alongside her.

"At some point," she recalled, "something miraculous happened to me on one of the week-long tours we took together. Everything magically fell into place."

"You had a pivotal moment."

"Yes, a very beautiful one, one that I wish for everyone with all my heart. It's not easy to describe." She closed her eyes briefly and let her horse lead her. "I think that, until then, all I saw in the wilderness was a wall of green and the sky and the mountains. Yeah, I heard the animal calls and smelled the scent of the wild, but they didn't tell me much. That day, however, I noticed how the veil in front of my eyes lifted and my senses sharpened. I began to perceive nature from the inside out. It was as though I'd passed through the gateway to a parallel world.

The diversity of life opened up to me on a spiritual level: smells, sounds, color spectra, air currents—everything was connected to everything else, and everything made sense. I was now connected to the wilderness and developed a strong sense of responsibility. I don't have any children... but I guess maybe that's how a mother feels."

Walker said nothing; he just stroked her arm gently.

Morning dawned. Lilly's trained eyes hardly missed anything. She pointed out wild boar tracks, deer and roe deer footprints, elk rubs and black bear claw marks. She noticed insects that camouflaged with the leaves they sat on and recognized every bird by its singing, trilling, whistling, chattering, chirping or scratching.

Being one-quarter Aborigine, Walker was familiar with that part of his family that still had access to the almost forgotten knowledge of the Australian Aborigines. Lilly listened intently as he talked about the skills of the trackers on the path they shared.

"Well into the nineteenth century, Aborigines lived completely isolated from the outside world. They could read footprints and other tracks like the characters of a script, and they'd use it all to put together a profile of the person or animal. They determined the age and sex, gait, direction, speed, and even purpose of the movement. It's pretty amazing. They even knew how each track might have been changed by the weather! And they interpreted smells and geological conditions and learned from insects and the smallest signs of plant life in the vicinity of the track. Some hunter-gatherers can still do this today, and we paleo-anthropologists try to use their skills in scientific tracking."

"I can imagine. Archaeology is also a search for clues."

"Indeed, it is. The knowledge of indigenous peoples opens many doors for us. You will certainly have heard of the San."

"The small hunter-gatherers in South West Africa."

"The oldest ethnic group on Earth and true masters of tracking. Not too long ago we flew three hunters from Namibia to southern France, where they helped us analyze seventeen-thousand-year-old human footprints in a cave. We wanted to know who the Stone Age people were, who left their footprints, and what they were doing. We assumed that the prints were made during dances."

"Were you right?" asked Lilly. "Waltz or foxtrot?"

Walker laughed. "You're funny, but actually we were proven wrong. The San hunters were phenomenal. They proceeded in a structured, almost scientific manner: question, investigation, hypothesis, verification, analysis, and conclusion. In the end, they could determine the number and gender of the Stone Age people from the proportions of the soles of their feet and their toes and then some: they calculated their age from cracks in the cornea of the heels and the position of the toes and their weight class from the surface shape and depth of the tracks. Then, the San determined their walking speed and posture. Seventeen thousand years later, mind you!"

"Unbelievable!" Lilly marveled. "So, what did the Stone Age people dance?"

Walker looked at her sheepishly. "Well, after the bushmen had discussed all the findings, they mutually agreed that the imprints... were probably made while mining clay."

Lilly laughed. "I've never heard of a dance like that."

Walker was getting at more. "If a few people still have such amazing abilities today... what would Neanderthals, who evolved independently over four hundred thousand years, be capable of?"

"Of things, I think, that we humans can hardly imagine. I was amazed to read about the Awa in the Brazilian rainforest. They shimmy through the treetops like monkeys and kill animals with their longbows. Try doing that!"

"Meanwhile we get frustrated if Instacart delivers our groceries an hour late. There are more people out there with superpowers, too. You may have heard of the Rarámuri people who live in the gorges and deserts of the Sierra Madre mountains in Mexico?"

Lilly shook her head.

"Well, you'll like this. See, they do their very own endurance training there. The men kick wooden balls in front of them for days in absurd games, covering hundreds of miles through rugged, high-altitude mountain areas."

"Tough guys."

"After my studies, I visited indigenous Thai people in the Andaman Sea, the semi-nomadic Moken. Their children live in their own universe, the sea. Their eyesight is fifty percent sharper than that of European children. Thanks to this acuity, they can spot their breakfast on the seabed without diving goggles."

"Fascinating! I suppose that's now part of their genome?"

"That's what I assume, just like the Bajau people in the Philippines, Malaysia, and Indonesia. Their divers can hold their breath for four minutes, sometimes more. They have developed a genetic ability to use oxygen more efficiently. Isn't it incredible?"

As the two continued to exchange stories as they walked, Stolin was only interested in wolf tracks. When the ground lay bare and soft, he searched it closely, knowing the prints would show more clearly there. He was mainly looking for the typical direct register trot, an easily recognizable feature whereby the wolf places its hind paws in the track of the front paws. But he didn't find anything. From time to time, he sucked sullenly on a bottle of whiskey, which didn't exactly improve his eyesight.

During a short break at a small mountain lake, Walker climbed up a rocky slope and disappeared into an inconspicuous rocky grotto that he had noticed from afar. On his return, he made a strange impression on Lilly but kept quiet about what he found inside. Under no circumstances was the trapper to find out. Only when they had been sitting in the saddle for some time, and Stolin had taken his whiskey moved away a little, did he hand her a flint wrapped in a handkerchief, which had been carved into an exemplary hand axe.

"Don't cut yourself," he warned her quietly, his eyes shining. "It's razor sharp!"

As the expedition progressed, it got frostier with every foot of altitude. It was still sunny, but when they had almost reached the summit of the next mountain, the weather changed abruptly. Gusty winds whipped fine ice crystals into their faces, and the visibility became increasingly limited. Stolin cursed his decision to come along.

Walker tied the three horses to his Mustang, grabbed the halter, and led the group forward through the snowstorm. He searched in vain for a hollow or an overhang beneath which they could take shelter. They could barely make out the terrain around them. They wandered disoriented through the wintry mountain landscape for several hours, gradually losing their bearings, but retaining a confidence that they would survive. Their clothing was functional, and their pockets were full of provisions. But where was the snowstorm driving them?

The young Australian's inner world of thought was just as turbulent as the outside world. A few hours ago, he had discovered a scientific sensation in a small, inconspicuous US cave. What he found was something no palaeoanthropologist had ever seen in this form. While ambitious excavators and archaeologists invested a tremendous amount of effort to brush sparse remains out of the dust of time, Walker was presented with a wholly preserved dwelling like a freshly laid table. Were it not for the axe he had taken with him, he might have assumed the whole scene had been some peculiar figment of his imagination, borne from hunger and the increasingly icy temperatures.

It was as if a self-reliant Stone Age cave dweller had left his quarters for the hunt just minutes before his arrival. His entire household was spread out on the floor: a cooled hearth with charred scraps of meat, a sleeping area furnished with animal skins and a work corner for making primitive tools and weapons. Walker saw half-finished leather garments, even jewelry made from red feathers and carnivore teeth. Intricate orange, red, black, and yellow animal paintings glowed on one wall. In a niche stood a small flute, similar to the thirty-five-thousand-year-old wind instrument made from the wing bone of a Griffon vulture found in the Hohle Fels Cave near Ulm, Germany, in 2009.

None of this was staged, however. It was real—something that Walker immediately realized, though could scarcely believe. If it were some complex field experiment, he would have known about it through his professional network. There was also the DNA analysis of the Neanderthal bone, the trail of which led to the vicinity of the Bitterroot Mountains. No other conclusion was possible: it had to be the temporary dwelling of a single existing Homo neanderthalensis, and if it existed, there would surely be others.

The existence of a last population of this archaic human form in the United States was inconceivable but entirely possible. Clovis, Folsom, and Nenana are officially considered to be the prehistoric cultures that mark the beginning of the colonization of the Americas, although some scientists have expressed doubts. These clans of hunter-gatherers lived in North America around twelve thousand years ago, and today's discovery would not change that. However, there was a completely different, more primitive form of human beings that colonized America, at least in places, and survived in an unknown terrain for thousands of years. Like the Clovis culture, maybe they migrated across the Bering Bridge from eastern Siberia to Alaska during or before the last glacial period and somehow managed to camouflage, conceal, and make themselves invisible to human civilization to this day.

The small cave was certainly not the place immortalized on the spearhead. Walker suspected the cave was just a base for the roaming Stone Age hunter hunting the Beringian wolf. Other Neanderthals could be somewhere deep in the mountains.

Was his home the mysterious place depicted by the engraving? He was more determined than ever to continue the search.

26

Stan woke up on the couch, looked at the clock, and realized he had to hurry. "Ten sharp! Work's calling, and I've got to go!" He woke Fred, who was snoring in the recliner, with a quick pat on the shoulder and warned him: "Don't get too close to him again. Keep your distance, man! He could have ripped off your arm if he wanted to."

Fred struggled to his feet. "Oh yeah, he could have. But he didn't. Don't worry! I'll call you when Ms. Feron gets back. Until then, we'd better keep this whole thing to ourselves." He accompanied the ranger to the door and watched him quickly clean his uniform before entering the car.

After Stan left, Fred felt lonely and uncomfortable, not only because he was ravenous but also because he now felt deep sympathy for the prisoner. It was heartbreaking to have him locked up like an animal, even though he had done nothing wrong.

To stave off hunger, he made himself a pizza. Omu ate nothing and drank nothing. He seemed to have resigned himself to the situation; his will seemed broken as he hunched over in the crate. He did not respond to Fred's words or offers. His elongated, enormous skull leaned against the bars, his eyes closed deep beneath the mighty bulges of bone, and his wide mouth bitterly contorted. Fred had never seen anything more miserable in his entire life. *When will Lilly be home?*

Somehow, he had to reach out to the sad inmate and invigorate him. But how? He switched on his cell phone. The home screen showed a mammoth fighting a pack of wolves. What would happen if he showed it to the primal creature in the cage? Then, he had an even better idea:

Go big or go home, he told himself, opened the laptop and searched for images of certain keywords, which he entered one after the other:

neanderthal, spear, Stone Age, mountains, wolf, hand axe

He loaded around twenty images into a separate file and placed the laptop on the floor in front of the cage, clearly visible to the prisoner but out of reach.

"Now look at that, my boy!"

The slide show was on a loop. One photo after another was displayed. It didn't take long for Omu to stir. He was fixated on the pictures. His astonishment was obvious, looped in confusion at how these familiar things were appearing before him as if in a dream. He tilted his head and grunted in amazement as he suspiciously observed the unfamiliar thing radiating bright pictures.

Soon, he was hanging from the bars, completely spellbound, trying to get as close as possible to the strange glowing window. Through it, he saw ghostly dream images of his kind and tools and weapons like those used by his people. Even wolves appeared before him, but they were motionless, as if frozen in ice. Like a child gazing into a kaleidoscope, all his worries seemed to fade away for a moment.

Fred whooped with joy at Omu's reaction. It had worked. The first step toward communication was a success. He pondered how he could build on this to initiate a dialogue with this exotic creature. Certainly, any kind of communication was of great benefit to everyone involved. There were so many questions and hardly any answers! Where had this Stone Age figure come from—someone Lilly Feron likely knew nothing about—and why was he stalking the wolf? The threads were tangled, everything bound together in ways he couldn't yet grasp. Or was he starting to? The mysterious spearhead that Stan had told him about seemed to be at the center of the whole mess. The Neanderthal wasn't after the wolf, otherwise he would have dragged it away. No, he apparently wanted to get his hands on this weapon.

Suddenly, Fred felt a vibration on his hip. The walkie-talkie! Lilly Feron liked these handheld radios. Small, inexpensive, and basically indestructible, you simply charge the battery and communicate effortlessly over six miles in any terrain.

Fred detached the buzzing device from his belt and looked at the display. *Oh dear, the Wolf Cub.* There was no way he could see what was going on in the office.

"Tom to base. Hellooo? Hi, hi. Tom to base. Hello, hello?"

"Base to Tom. It's me, Fred. I'm holding down the fort here. What's up, Tom? Everything okay with you? Over."

"Roger. Hi, hi. Hellooo? Hello, Fred. Just visited the small enclosure. Everything is fine. Then I remembered something, Fred."

"What's that, Tom?"

"Lilly did say... well, she did say... that the timber wolves would get the worming treatment this week... well, they should get it!"

Fred remembered. "Roger. Tom, you're great. That's right! I'd forgotten all about it. Man, you're clever! So, you need the pills then, right? You want to put them into the wolves' mouths, right? Over and out."

"Hi, hi. Exactly. Can you give them to me? I'm just outside the entrance. Why don't you bring them out for me so I don't get everything dirty again? I was in the forest. There's a lot of mud. And cleaning is *sooo* boring!"

"Roger, yes, that it is, definitely!"

That's how Tom was. He stood outside the front door and called Fred on his walkie-talkie. He could have rung the doorbell.

"It's all right, Tom! Stay where you are! Do you want to put them in chicken livers again? I can get you a pack from the freezer. Over."

"Yes, chicken liver is good. Chicken liver. That would be great! Delicious! Then they'll be gone in no time."

"Roger. I'll be with you in a minute. Just wait outside, Tom! I'll be right there. Over."

Meanwhile, the slide show had brought Omu out of his lethargy. He was awake, alert, and listening attentively to the hissing and crackling of the radio conversation. He realized that the redhead was communicating with an imaginary person and watched him remove a package of frozen food from the freezer. Not even the smallest detail escaped him—including what Fred did afterwards:

Diagonally opposite the crate stood Lilly Feron's green medicine fridge which she always kept locked and in which she kept antibiotics, painkillers, vaccines, vitamins, and other substances. The redhead pulled out his keychain and opened the padlock on the cupboard door. Omu watched the process carefully. It was quick, but he saw the shiny key slide into the lock and turn. He heard the metallic click and watched as the bobo removed the lock, opened the door, and put the keychain back into his pocket. He understood that the green box could be opened in this way. Bobo rummaged around in it, took some things out, and carried them outside.

Alone in the room, Omu suddenly reached for the padlock on the crate door. It looked exactly the same as the one that was attached to the green box. He thought hard. The laptop was only three steps away from the cage. He quickly untied the leather strap around his waist and deftly knotted a loop from it. He then stretched his arm out of the bars as far as he could and threw the loop from his wrist like a lasso over Fred's computer. Now he could carefully pull the thing toward him. When it was within reach, he untied the loop, tied the strap back on, lay on his side, and closed his eyes.

Breathing in and out calmly, he waited for Fred to return. *Come on, bobo!*

Once the wind finally died down, it soon stopped snowing. The bright midday sun crept steadily over the rugged mountain peaks and shone into the valley. The air was clear and cool, and the inclement weather had passed.

Lilly gave Walker an enamored look. He had guided the riders and horses without incident, even if they didn't know exactly where they were going. No one had fallen, and, most importantly, no horse had been injured. Slightly chilled and exhausted, they desperately needed to take a break, eat, and change out of their damp clothes. They found a suitable spot at the edge of a forest where there was grass and melting water for the horses.

After changing her clothes, Lilly used a gas burner to brew coffee. From the backpacks, she dug out salted almonds, tomato soup, fruit juice and venison jerky.

Walker placed his Akubra to dry in the sun and sat down beside her. The coffee felt incredibly good. He stroked Lilly's back. Then, he slowly opened a pocket on his vest and cautiously pulled out the spearhead that he had brought from the laboratory. He kissed Lilly on the forehead and carefully hung it around her neck.

"This thing is magical, just like you. Take good care of it!"

Moved by the unexpected display of trust, Lilly hugged him. She quickly hid the spearhead under her T-shirt. It felt as if it radiated a mystical, soothing power that reverberated through her bones. She reached for Walker's hand and placed it gently on her chest, allowing him to feel the pendant and her heartbeat all at once.

In the distance, Stolin trudged along in a foul mood, map in hand, twisting and turning, muttering curses as the landscape stubbornly refused to match the confusing lines on the paper. It was amusing to watch him. He couldn't work out where he was, which drove him crazy. The fact that his whiskey bottle was empty save for a few final shots did little to help.

His companions, from whom he increasingly distanced himself inwardly, were solely to blame. In his delusion, he blamed them for being stuck and for everything else, including the bad weather and the lack of alcohol. As he saw it, the two naïve adventurers had lured him into the wasteland and seduced him into taking a risk he knew to be unwise. It was only because of the damned wolf fur that he had allowed himself to listen to them. He had always avoided the Bermuda Mountains, and now he was right in the middle of the damned place. He cursed the map, the expedition, the Beringian wolf, and the merciless wilderness that now held him in its fierce stranglehold.

Panting, his hunting rifle slung over his shoulder, he climbed up a rocky hill where he hoped to get a better panoramic view. When he reached the top, he realized the view here was also restricted by dense forest, scree, and steep rock faces. Only another hill with three giant trees could be seen from here. Did it continue there? Would anyone hear his shot in this godforsaken place? Without thinking, he took his hunting rifle from his shoulder, released the safety catch, and fired two clean shots into the air. The deafening bangs rebounded a dozen times on the craggy rock faces and abruptly silenced the birds' pleasurable midday calls.

"What an idiot," Lilly hissed. "And that's what they call a gamekeeper!"

"Please don't do that, Mr. Stolin," Walker called to him, feigning a relaxed tone. "We'll never find the wolf that way. And apart from the Beringian wolf, nobody will hear it anyway."

Lilly almost exploded, but she pulled herself together. "I wouldn't be surprised if the moron made a run for it. Not that I'd mind one bit."

"Agree!" Walker laid his cheek against hers and murmured: "In the cave... I made an incredible discovery there."

"Yes, you found this hand axe."

"Much more than that. A complete dwelling."

"The dwelling of an early human?"

"Yes. You can't imagine how I feel. I'm playing it cool in front of that wacko, but I'm shaking inside. All my life, I've been dealing with old things, ancient, bygone things that are barely tangible. And now, I'm looking into this grotto... and into the living room of a living Neanderthal, into his daily existence. I still can't believe it!"

"That means they really do exist!"

"He exists. We don't know if there are any more."

"But that's obvious."

"Yes, Lilly. There can't be many, a few hundred at most; otherwise, it would have been known by now. They would have been exposed long ago, harassed by researchers, and besieged by the press. You know how it gets."

"That makes sense. Their strategic advantage is that they are a manageable population that knows how to hide well. It all seems so logical now."

"They have a clear advantage out here. It's their terrain. They are certainly smarter than any animal or human in the wild. But where are they hiding?" Walker looked over at Frank Stolin, three hundred feet away, still grumbling, the map in one hand and a marching compass in the other. "I've been thinking about it, Lilly. Whether we find them or not, we should keep it to ourselves. We have to protect them. We mustn't betray them."

Walker didn't want to rush headlong into things and publicize this sensation, but Frank Stolin was a real problem. He didn't seem trustworthy. The trapper didn't know everything yet. How would he react? Anything could happen. However, parting ways with this man in the middle of nowhere was not an option either. They had to get along somehow.

As if she had read his thoughts, Lilly whispered in Stolin's direction: "He's unpredictable. We have to be careful." Worried, she snuggled closer against Walker's broad shoulder.

The day was still long. They decided to rest briefly and then ride on. Walker lit a small fire. For his midday nap, Stolin drank whiskey and made a camp under a rocky overhang. Lilly brought him toasted rusks and a tin cup of hot tomato soup. He pretended to be asleep. She knew he was pretending.

Lilly had spotted wolf tracks before they reached the rest area but had kept it to herself. Now, she asked Walker to accompany her and use the time to set up three game cameras near the tracks. The waterproof cameras would capture everything that moved in front of them at any time of day for up to six months, automatically recording high-resolution images and videos. Lilly would then analyze the data, waiting for the sight she craved.

An hour later, they returned to the camp. Just as Lilly had suspected, Stolin was gone. Apart from his riding horse, he took the packhorse and most of the provisions. The shards of a shattered whiskey bottle lay scattered around his camp, and Jolly Rancher wrappers hung in the branches of the bushes. He was trying to get by on his own. What was he up to? Was he heading back to Painted Rocks Lake, or was he going after the Beringian wolves? Lilly could only hope that he hadn't spotted any more of them. Horrified, she imagined one of the rare animals tied to his packhorse as a hunting trophy.

Walker also feared more trouble. He didn't want to imagine an encounter between the drunken trapper and a Neanderthal. What chance would the latter have against a hunter with a modern hunting rifle?

"He's a madman, Lilly. We need to follow him."

Lilly recognized that hoof prints led up the stone hill from where the trapper had fired the shot a day earlier. They quickly packed up their equipment, tied the remaining bags behind the saddles, and followed the trail.

From the top of the hill, they had a spectacular view of another hilltop a few hundred feet away, with three magnificent pine trees enthroned on its summit. Their colossal trunks, around five feet thick, towered over two hundred feet into the air, an imposing sight in the spacious, barren landscape.

"Three ancient western American larches," exclaimed Lilly excitedly. "The tallest trees in Montana, you know. These must be a thousand years old."

The closer they got, the more obvious it became that the three lonely giants could be seen from a great distance in almost every direction. Walker dismounted, handed Lilly the reins, and ran his hand over the purple-gray bark with its deep, wide cracks and dry scales. Further up, the bark of the thick branches glowed a bright orange-brown. Lilly tilted her head back to see jackdaws demonstrating their flying skills in the treetops. The sprawling, shaggy canopy of the conifers looked like a whole forest.

"Three giant larches you can't miss are an excellent landmark," Walker said, opening the image of the spearhead engraving on his phone and looking around thoughtfully. He concentrated on the structures around the three engraved cones, wandered around, and scanned the surroundings for similarities. Finally, he walked a few steps around a small rock and called out: "There's a path here with a similar curve. That could be it."

Lilly immediately rode toward him with the horses. She discovered Stolin's tracks. "Let's go!"

The ground was initially earthy and damp from the previous day's rainfall. This made it easy for them to recognize footprints. When the sparse vegetation gave way to bare rocks and the ground became stony, the trail ended. Nevertheless, they rode ahead without hesitating, as Stolin's direction of travel was clear. The path had no branches or alternative routes; there was only one way forward or back. On one side, it became increasingly steep; on the other, rock piled higher and higher. With each minute they rode, the path narrowed, meandering past a steep rock face on the right while the slope fell away to the left.

When the horses began to resist, the riders dismounted and led them on foot. They were almost considering turning back when they heard the clattering of hooves. It could only be Frank Stolin. He was already running around the bend toward them like a thief caught in the act. His head was hanging down, and the kidnapped horses were tied one behind the other. A pitiful sight!

"That's the end back there," he shouted hoarsely. "You have to turn back. It's a dead end. Now turn around!"

Walker didn't want any bickering or the matter to escalate, but he still vented his displeasure: "You could have woken us up. Now you see that you can't get far on your own."

"Where does the path lead to?" asked Lilly, iron-willed.

"I told you, ma'am, no way forward," came the defiant reply.

"What did you see?"

"The path leads into a basin. There's a lake and lots of vegetation, surrounded by high rock faces. Perhaps it is very nice and romantic for lovebirds like you. But that's it. End of the line! It's not going anywhere, get it?"

"A mountain lake? How far is it?" Walker asked coolly.

"Five minutes on foot. Why?"

"How big is the lake?"

"Maybe three hundred and thirty feet in diameter. A waterfall feeds it. Nothin' else there. A spooky, lonely place. Just leave it alone! It's a dead end. The end of the world. Don't you understand?"

Walker sought Lilly's gaze again. They were both thinking the same: a still body of water of this size enclosed in steeply sloping terrain. The description matched the symbol on the engraving and its counterpart on the map.

"Is there a stream?" the Australian inquired.

"No. I don't know where the water from the waterfall goes. Into the underground, I guess."

"That could be good," said the professor, breaking a piece of crumbly rock out of the rock face beside him. "There's a lot of soft, soluble limestone here. Water could easily seep into this stuff. I've been thinking about it for a while."

"What are you thinking about, man?"

"I think the whole region here is a glaciokarst."

"A what?"

"We are in a formerly frozen karst landscape. During the Ice Age, North America was partly covered by glaciers. Where there was soft and brittle limestone, the ice masses eroded it. Water washed it out from below. Entire mountain peaks collapsed. This is how funnel-shaped depressions were formed a long time ago. Some of these sinkholes are over two thousand feet deep and even larger in diameter."

Lilly was familiar with this and joined in with his explanation: "Geologists also call them dolines. I've explored one before. They are so interesting for biologists because they are isolated habitats with their own ecosystems."

"Ecosystem? I don't give a shit!" Stolin scoffed. "Damn ecosystems!"

"Careful!" Walker warned him sharply.

The trapper flinched.

For the first time, Lilly saw Walker angry. "Which side was the waterfall on?" she asked.

"Right. It's on the right."

Walker looked at his cell phone. "Right behind it is the human symbol."

Stolin laughed bitterly. "A stick figure isn't a waterfall. So, forget it! Whatever it is you're looking for, it's not there."

"You could be right," Lilly soothed the irritated trapper. She grabbed Walker's hand and pulled him away with her. A few steps away, she hugged him and whispered in his ear, "Unless there's more beyond the waterfall!"

That didn't seem unrealistic. Walker knew that individual sinkholes are often connected to others via cave systems, and it was possible that another one was connected to the first.

Stolin was increasingly exasperated. "Listen, leave me alone with all your crap! We're ridin' back right now. Because what I haven't told you is that the horses got very uneasy at the lake."

"Uneasy? Why?"

The trapper sat down at the side of the path, looking miserable and tired. "There were strange sounds," he said muffled. "I didn't know where they were coming from. Apparently, they were from everywhere."

"Like echoes bouncing from the rock faces?"

"Yes, echoes everywhere. I almost thought they were human sounds. Creepy human voices. Very spooky sounds. Believe me, they were damn ghostly! They came from everywhere, minglin' with the sound of the waterfall. But you couldn't see nothing. And then the horses panicked."

"Panicked? Like when you met the Beringian wolf?" Stolin's fearful expression answered Lilly's question.

Walker adjusted his Akubra. "I think we'll take a look for ourselves. You can turn around and ride to Painted Rocks Lake, Mr. Stolin. We won't hold it against you."

Peeved, the trapper watched as the two unsaddled their horses and tied them to a large stone.

Lilly patted her Morgan mare on the neck. "We've come a long way with you. We'll do the last bit on foot. Be good! We'll be back soon."

They unbuckled their luggage, packed a minimal amount of equipment into a small backpack and set off. Stolin couldn't understand why neither of them had taken a weapon with them.

"Without a gun?" he called after him dismissively. "You're not taking a gun with you? That's what I call courage!"

"I have a knife," Walker replied unconcernedly. "I'm good with it."

"Oh, a knife! For making sandwiches?" Stolin mocked. "I've had enough of this! I'm stayin' here, waitin' for you to come back tomorrow morning. If you don't come, you're dead and I'm gone!"

They didn't respond. He watched in consternation as they walked lightly along the steep slope around the high wall until they were out of sight.

28

Here he lies, the proud hunter, caught like a cottontail rabbit in a trap. Omu is desperate. Without the spearhead, his people are in danger. Whoever has it can find the way to the primeval valley, to his Kela and all his brothers and sisters. This must not happen! It would be the end for them… they can't exist anywhere else. He will never give up; he will bring the spearhead home. This is his duty, his path.

Omu does not move. The bait is laid out, and the illuminated picture window is within reach. He pretends to be asleep. After a while, he hears the returning man's footsteps. When the redhead stops in the room, Omu feels his gaze resting on him. He is surprised that the picture window is so close to the cage. The man pauses to consider what he should do and whether he should dare grab it and take it.

Do it. Come here. I am waiting!

Resting and with closed eyes, the hunter pauses until his victim approaches the picture window like an unsuspecting carp in a weir. Soon, he is right there. Omu can smell his breath, hear his anxious heart pounding, and the rustling of his clothing as the man stretches out his arm to grab the thing.

This is the moment!

Quick as a flash, Omu grabs his forearm once again and pulls him through the bars up to his shoulder. Bobo screams like an impaled raccoon. The shiny keychain—Omu's treasure—rattles in his clothes. With his free hand, he reaches out through the bars and takes it from the stranger's pocket. While he mercilessly clamps the redhead's arm with his foot, he calmly opens the cage. Then, he releases the raccoon and leaps out of the den like a marten.

When bobo almost reaches his feet with a sore arm, Omu stands over him and pushes him down quickly. He won't hurt him; he only wants to know one simple thing:

Where is the spearhead?

The trainee sat on the cold floor in Lilly's office with a dislocated shoulder, lamenting himself for surrendering without a fight. The Stone Age man had caught him off guard for the second time. *How stupid can I be?*

He looked up at the victor with the expression of a defeated man, convinced that he was finally in for it. *Make it short*, Fred thought. But, in reality, he saw no hostility, only gentleness in the massive visage above him. *Was the overpowering bundle of muscle offering him his hand out of pity?* Spontaneously, he reached out and cried out in pain as Omu pulled him up toward him—his shoulder!

His counterpart, only a little smaller than him, smelled of musk and animal droppings and held his hand in an iron grip. Resistance was futile!

"What do you want?" Fred shouted desperately, knowing full well that Omu didn't understand. "You twisted my arm!"

As if he had understood anyway, the Neanderthal sighed sympathetically and began to gently palpate Fred's upper and lower arm. He carefully bent the joints back and forth, examining him almost like an orthopedic surgeon. The injured man silently endured everything.

Omu sighed once more, then firmly grabbed Fred's armpit with one hand and jerked his arm with the other. Before he realized what was happening, his shoulder joint was locked back into place with a hollow crack. It happened so quickly that there was no time to cry out in pain. Pleasantly surprised, he allowed himself to be moved toward the settee, where he willingly dropped into an armchair. It hardly hurt, and all his bones seemed to return where they belonged. "Well done. You fixed me."

Omu stood before him with his legs apart, grinning bizarrely and thumping his chest proudly. "Omu," he said. "Omu."

So that was his name. Fred didn't hesitate to tell him his name, and he succeeded.

"Frett, Frett, Frett!" Omu repeated as he moved into the eating area.

The trainee followed him and saw the Neanderthal looking through the large panoramic window. Was there anything else he wanted to tell him?

Omu pointed from himself to the forest that surrounded the courtyard. He wanted to go outside. Now, he pointed at Fred and indicated with a downward palm that he should stay there. He made this gesture several times as he walked backward, step by step. "Galu! Galu!" he said, tilting his head and watching Fred's reaction.

Fred understood the sign language intuitively. Omu wanted to go out, and Fred was supposed to wait for him here. *In his language*, Fred thought, *galu must mean something like stay or wait.*

Agreeing, Fred pointed to himself, repeated the staying gesture, and spoke: "Okay, galu. Fred galu." Again he resented his own submissiveness, but he couldn't tame or restrain the wild man. Putting him on a leash and taking him for a walk wasn't an option either... after all, this is man, not dog. Because he wanted to play it safe, he just kept talking. "No problem, Omu. I'll wait. I'll galu. I'll stay here. I'll wait for you. That's perfectly all right. Frett galu. Don't worry! Just make sure nobody catches you out there; otherwise, we'll both be in big trouble!"

Slightly amused by the torrent of words, Omu gurgled out funny sounds and grimaced with satisfaction. Then, he returned to the office, gathered his rudimentary hunting gear, strapped on his flint knife and reached for his pouches. Before disappearing, he made the stay gesture again, said, "Frett galu," then moved backward to the front door, fumbling around with the handle until the door burst open. He had already disappeared.

Fred sat dutifully in the armchair and tried to process what had happened. *Does the Neanderthal really know my name now? How long will he stay away? Is all this just a trick to get as far away as possible? He's cunning enough!* Either way, Fred knew he had no choice but to wait. He took a deep breath, tried to relax, and closed his eyes.

Omu was standing against the wall opposite him when he came back around. He had been fast asleep. Dazed, he watched as the hunter pulled his flint knife from its leather holster and, with a few well-directed cuts, scratched the outline of what he was looking for into the plaster in front of him: an important spear. The long shaft and the distinctively shaped spearhead, which was the spearhead Lilly possessed, were visible. She had what the wild man wanted. Fred wanted him to understand that his boss would return and that Omu only had to wait for her. Maybe now the communication could work.

"Omu, you're looking for that spearhead, right?" he said calmly, pointing to the mural. "Good, I want to help you with that. I *can* help you."

The Neanderthal looked at him inquiringly. Fred took his cell phone and opened the pictures he had taken at the accident scene. Omu gaped speechlessly at the photos, the dead Beringian wolf on the side of the road and the blonde woman in another shot.

"This is Lilly. Lilly, my boss. Lilly Feron. She's got the thing you are looking for," he said, pointing to the spearhead on the wall, and then back at Lilly's photograph. He made an effort to illustrate that his treasure was in her possession. "Lilly's got it! She's coming back. Omu, wait for her! Omu galu! You have to wait for her here. Galu!"

Omu seemed to understand. He showed a restrained, hopeful grin that exposed his big yellow teeth. "Omu galu," he grumbled calmly, reaching for the hunting pouch he had carried on the short walk through the forest. He knelt before Fred and pulled out a damp brown lump of clay that he had dug up. He skillfully pressed a hollow into it, into which he scattered arnica flowers and a bitter herb. As nimble as a baker, he rolled and kneaded the mixture vigorously and formed it into a plate the size of the palm of his hand. He slipped the fragrant packet under Fred's T-shirt and pressed it gently against his shoulder.

The patient willingly tolerated it. "Very diplomatic! You're helping me because I'm helping you."

The healing clay warmed up after a short time and took effect. The pain subsided. A joyful gurgling sound from Omu's throat indicated his inner satisfaction at what he had achieved. He had plenty of reasons for this: he had deceived, tricked and taken the redhead by surprise, escaped from the cell, unintentionally injured him in the process, and then examined him and given him medical treatment. To his great delight, Fred had told him that the woman with the sun hair would bring the engraved spearhead to them. Rewarding himself for all this, Omu unwrapped the raw herb meat and ate it eagerly.

They were both dead tired. Omu crawled behind the living room sofa, and Fred fell asleep in the armchair.

30

Kela had successfully chased away one foolish bobo when she was startled by the footsteps of two more intruders. She immediately dropped her tools, moved close to the falling water, and peered out through the haze.

There they are in the warm afternoon light by the lake, just a few steps away from her: a dark, curly-haired man and a light-haired woman. Kela is worried. Scaring away the lone bobo and the horses didn't help. Now, more have arrived.

Through the haze of water, she observes them closely: their gestures, facial expressions, posture, and clothing. Something deep inside her tells her that these graceful bobos pose no danger. They feel different to the other one. They are unarmed and seem to be searching for something. The eyes in their strange, flat faces seem peaceful and warm.

They get closer to the waterfall and closer to Kela. She doesn't move. She notices the man's shell jewelry. The light-haired bobo woman is also wearing something on her chest.

When standing at arm's length from her and Merely a bit of water separates them, Kela recognizes the object around her neck.

The sight of her ancestor's engraved spearhead hits her with the force of a stone club. Omu himself should have returned with the treasure of her people, but now Kela knows that the spearhead with its secret markings has fallen into the wrong hands. An icy feeling of helplessness overcomes her. What can she do? They are already too close; it is too late to use the spirit voices.

Pushing forward, the stranger stretches her slender arm through the falling water. Her hand is delicate and filigree. The spray splashes off her fine, *smooth skin in glistening pearls. Then, the light-haired woman takes a deep breath and takes another step forward. Suddenly drenched, she feels around and strides forward until finally standing in the dry, gloomy, rocky cave.*

She opens her astonished, green eyes that radiate enchantment, not fear.

Kela feels her mild gaze and senses the aura of this impressive, slender woman, whose small, cute mouth smiles peacefully at her.

31

She emerged from nowhere, bare-chested, a faint dusting of hair on her face catching the light, a stone axe swinging low at her hips. Time seemed to shudder; Lilly's breath caught, her heart stuttered—but she forced herself to stand tall, meeting the stranger's gaze with as much calm and quiet benevolence as she could summon.

Even more than the stocky physique, the wolf expert was captivated by the facial expression of this peculiar-looking woman, who was only four foot three. Like the exaggerated expressions of a caricature, different emotions seemed to be superimposed in the purest form: sheer despair and hopelessness stood out, but Lilly also read genuine warmth and kindness in the strange human-like creature. Its gnarled, elongated skull, which lacked a chin and forehead, resembled a roughly carved Halloween mask from which two small, sparkling hawk eyes stared incessantly at Lilly's necklace.

Now, Walker had also penetrated the rushing curtain. He rubbed the water from his eyes and realized he was in a shadowed grotto, a hollow some five hundred square feet wide tucked behind the waterfall. On the opposite side of the cave was a glaringly bright passageway, a window to the outside world that dazzled him like a bright spotlight. He stepped up and looked through it. He would never forget what he saw:

Like a romantic painting framed by the stone opening, an enchanting wooded valley opened up before him. Stately sequoias over three hundred and thirty feet high, giant larches, and Sitka spruces formed the canopy of the paradisiacal basin. Between them grew smaller deciduous trees, old cypresses, man-sized ferns, climbing plants and colorful bushes. Jeffrey and Ponderosa pines were scattered on the dry limestone slopes at the sinkhole's edge. The blue sky was visible here and there, and in a handful of places, the sun's rays shone through the treetops and illuminated colorful clearings and a sparkling stream.

Overwhelmed by the sight, the Australian leaned forward to get a better view of the scene. As far as he could see, the entire area was surrounded by steep rock faces towering over twenty-three hundred feet high. At the foot of the cliffs, one grotto followed the next in a ring. Were they used as dwellings? In the distance, children played on the banks of the stream. Like music in a concert hall, the birdcalls and animal songs of the forest could be heard clearly.

"That's it, Lilly. This is the place on the engraving," he said as if in a trance. "It's an ancient giant sinkhole. It's so beautiful. This is where they live, hence the human symbol."

Only when he turned around did Walker realize that they were not alone. Standing opposite Lilly in the semi-darkness at the edge of the cavity was the stocky, broad-chested figure, which the palaeoanthropologist promptly identified as a Neanderthal woman. At first, he saw her as a threat. He suddenly flinched and struggled to suppress a silent scream. The hominid immediately fixed her eyes on him, turned slowly in his direction, ducked like a wild cat preparing to pounce and nimbly reached for the stone axe on her leather belt.

At that moment, Lilly addressed the little hominid in a warm and friendly voice: "We have something for you here." Leisurely and with stoic calm, she slipped the necklace over her head and held it out to the Stone Age woman with both hands. Like a humble she-wolf, Lilly bowed slightly and demonstratively made herself small in front of her.

Walker intuitively adopted a similar stance. That seemed to ease the situation. The half-naked woman hesitantly let go of the axe and turned her attention back to Lilly and the pendant that enthralled her. Tilting her head, she examined the piece of jewelry like a child whose mother was giving a long-awaited gift. Suspiciously, she took another look at the strange human figures, who she now realized likely posed her no threat. Then, she plucked up her courage and grabbed it quickly. Whimpering softly, she pressed the engraved spearhead to her bosom, sank to the ground, and looked at it wistfully.

"Omu," she said in a soft, sonorous voice. "Ugunu Omu," and her melancholy words mingled with the steady rushing of the waterfall.

The tension eased. Lilly took a deep breath. The whole situation seemed so surreal that she giggled, involuntarily and childlike. As their eyes met, Walker also had to smile, mostly because—despite all his previous knowledge—the Neanderthal woman was even less attractive than he could ever have imagined. When the hominid joined in, giggling strangely, the trio laughed so heartily together that all apprehension left them.

After the laughter faded, the little archaic woman began an enchanting performance. She used the grotto as a stage and began gesticulating and playfully showing what was important to her. Walker and Lilly listened with fascination to the torrent of grunts, vocalizations, and clicks in which the word "Omu" kept recurring. What she was saying was completely unintelligible, but the structure and complexity of her expression kept them intensely engaged.

Walker found himself pondering how language, as we know it today, is thought to have only come into being around twenty thousand years ago, when our ancestors learned to combine words in different ways. Since most paleoanthropologists assume that the last Neanderthals died out over thirty-five thousand years ago, they believe that this form of human, as long as it existed, communicated in a primitive way absent of grammar. Since this Neanderthal's clan had had time to evolve their language to the present, Walker assumed their chatter followed a structure much like other modern tongues. Only it sounded utterly alien.

The anatomy of the vocal apparatus played an essential role in the sound of their vocalizations. The hominid's sounds in her larynx, pharynx, mouth and nose were just as peculiar and bizarre as her rustic appearance. However, although Walker did not understand the individual syllables, he was sure she had a sophisticated command of language. Even to Lilly, who did not claim to match the professor's expertise in this field, it was indisputable that these were not inarticulate sounds like those made by animals. The Neanderthal woman demonstrated that her clan could use language to convey knowledge, tell stories, and refer to other times and specific places; they could create and understand new expressions, talk about the language, and even lie.

"Could an understanding be possible between her and us?" Lilly asked the room.

"Yes," Walker promptly assured. "The ability to learn foreign languages is also one of the characteristics of human language. And this beauty here can speak."

"Indeed," Lilly agreed.

Now, the creature patted her chest with both hands and repeated her own name several times: "Kela, Kela, Kela!"

"Okay. You are Kela. I am Walker. Walker. This here is Lilly. Lilly."

"Warka, Lily," Kela repeated.

They had introduced themselves and were happy about it.

"And who is Omu?" Lilly repeated the word she had heard several times. "Omu?"

Kela seemed overcome with melancholy again, but she collected herself, paced expressively back and forth between the stone culvert and the waterfall and performed a delightful pantomime. First, she played the hunter, sneaking up and throwing a spear. Then, she imitated the prey, a panting quadruped; it must have been a wolf.

"Omu is the name of the hunter who wounded the wolf," exclaimed Lilly in surprise.

When the Neanderthal finally crouched down, put her head on her knees and spoke the name longingly, it became clear that she missed her beloved Omu.

They had understood Kela. Lilly crouched next to her and stroked her comfortingly. This woman could be her friend, and Lilly was desperate to protect her.

32

"*Galu-tsi-tet-k!*"

Kela does not know if the foolish intruders understand her order to stay and wait. As different and ugly as they seem to her, she has come to trust them.

"*Galu-tsi-tet-k,*" *she repeats her request and makes a well-meaning gesture to sit down on the rocky cave floor. The dark man and the white woman seem to understand and sit down. That's good.*

Kela rolls through the stone arch into the flickering light of the primeval valley and runs down the gravel path that has been trodden for a thousand years, past the grottoes of the blue tribe, where it smells of meat, roots, mushrooms and herbs. The blues are the hunter-gatherers of their people, strong and fast. Mastering camouflage, they are allowed into the outside world to hunt and forage for food in the shelter of the vast forests, including birch bark for making sticky tar, quartzite and pebbles for tools and much more for living and hunting. The Blue tribe is one of the five tribes of their people.

Kela chooses the path down to the stream, calling out words of warning to children scuffling on the bank; she knows every one of them. Those of the White tribe painted with bright lime protect the young. The whites are the caretakers who look after the young, weak, old and sick sisters and brothers.

Kela hastily wades through the cool stream, jumps down the embankment, and dips into the old grove in the center of the valley. This is the forest that her people preserve, honor, and respect. Kela could traverse it even if she were blind; she knows it so well. The green tribe preserves it, preventing every fire, every clearcutting, and every destruction of the plant kingdom.

She is already crossing the dense forest's small and large clearings and paradisiacal gardens. Some are populated by members of the red tribe, to which

Kela also belongs. The reds are the producers in the area. They sow and harvest wild oats and keep wild boar, forest rabbits and black-tailed hares in cages. They increase what they have and store it for bad times when hunter-gatherers return home empty-handed. The reds encourage the exchange of produce among the tribes. What gatherers bring, producers multiply, and what the yellow craftsmen work on should benefit everyone equally.

Kela has arrived at Hani's tent. He is the eldest of the Red tribe, clever, good, and wise, and one of the five tribal leaders.

"Jitti-bij-kat-zu-chucka—the spearhead is back!" she calls from afar, clicking and clicking so loudly that several sisters and brothers run to her excitedly and gaze in amazement at the engraved spearhead around her neck.

"You have the spearhead! Where is the spear? Where's Omu?" asks Hani when he sees it.

Out of breath, Kela greets him and kisses his hand with reverence. Beaming with joy, she recounts what has happened and tells him about her encounter with the two bobos. Hani listens to her patiently.

"May these strangers be allowed in?" Kela asks him pleadingly.

Hani closes his eyes and remains deeply introspective until he replies: "It's good that the engraved spearhead has returned. It is understandable, Kela, that you trust these bobos. But the law of our people does not allow intruders—you know that."

"Yes, Hani, but they are good and could be useful to us. I can feel it. They brought the spearhead to us, and I hope Omu is still alive. Maybe we can find him... with their help."

Hani closes his eyes again, pauses and thinks. "All right," he finally says. "Give me a piglet. We'll take it to the Yellow tribe, then to the Blue one. There, we will ask the elders!"

A Neanderthal woman brings Hani a securely tied piglet with a carrying handle. They set off immediately.

The numerous caves of the yellow tribe are located deep in the steep walls on the remote side of the sinkhole, opposite the stone arch. Like the red and blue tribes, the yellow has its own tasks. They are craftsmen who create clothing, tools, weapons, fish traps, and other equipment. They are inventive and dexterous. They trade their goods for oats, fresh hunting spoils, and forest fruits; trading benefits everyone.

Kela has to wait outside under the canopy while Hani talks to Taku, the elder of the yellow tribe—Hani hands Taku the piglet, who squeals loudly. An old Neanderthal woman takes away the gift.

Voices and the rhythmic sounds of craftsmanship resound from the workshops. Kela was often there and acquired skills that Omu admired in her. Before his hunting test, she eagerly created soft leather clothing for him, which she had previously tanned with rhubarb roots and oak bark and made waterproof by smoking it. She also made moccasins padded with straw and fur and a pouch of rabbit skin, which she filled with provisions and everything he needed for the journey. The evening before his departure, she presented him with these gifts and swore her eternal devotion to him.

The great festival of colors had already been prepared to honor Omu, the new leader. But he and the spear had not returned. The tribal leaders came together and consulted. Kela's people could live with the loss of a warrior; as painful as it was, they would get over it, but never before had the engraved spearhead been out of their possession. Each day they waited, the hope of its return dwindled, and the fear of being discovered grew among the color tribes.

After many days of darkness, the fire of hope is burning in Kela today. When Hani and Taku approach her, she recognizes the same glimmer of hope on their faces.

"It's good," says Taku. "Gora from the white tribe and Cina from the green tribe will be notified. We'll all gather with the Old Watka. She is to decide, for she is our oldest gatherer and the link to the outside world where the bobos live. Everyone reveres her. I will also present her with a gift."

It's not far from Old Watka. She is sitting by a gnarled, ancient cedar tree, where a flock of parrots has taken up residence. She cracks pecan nuts with her mouth and tells children stories from the wilderness, of the snow-covered mountains, of lynxes and hawks and of wild herbs and medicinal mushrooms. Watka is their queen bee; the old and young buzz around her day in and day out, caring for her and asking her questions. She guards the knowledge of her people and passes it on every day:

yarrow prevents inflammation; ribwort plantain helps with healing; the root of the daylily is delicious; wild roses are also a source of food in winter; all the other knowledge that makes the survival of the clan possible.

When Kela and the four elders reach the cedar tree, Watka ends her story by throwing two handfuls of pecan nuts far behind the young audience. The children and parrots happily set about collecting them.

The visitors reverently sit in the vacant area before the gatherer. They respect her because she has more insight into the big world than all of them together. Not even the slightest thing seems to escape her watchful eyes.

"Weren't you with me just yesterday, Hani, to show me two young ice wolves?" the old woman asks somewhat brusquely and then continues in a friendlier tone, "I was pleased. This kind of wolf has become rare. The pups are starving, but they will regain their strength. Gali is taking care of them and giving them boar's milk and pieces of liver."

"That's good, Watka," smiles the red-faced Hani. "The two orphans were close to death. They can regain their strength here in the valley. Then the hunters will return them to the wild."

Taku, his face glowing in bright yellow ochre, opens a small, finely carved wooden box, sticks his index and middle fingers inside and paints Watka's forehead with intense blue paint. He then hands her the tin and bows respectfully. "May your face shine like the cloudless summer sky. Our best lapis lazuli blue is my gift to you, great Watka."

The old woman bows in turn. "You have made good use of the stones my gatherers brought you. The blue will make my face glow like wild blueberries."

The leaders of the green and white tribes also appeared with gifts. Gora gives the old gatherer a dried Lingzhi medicinal mushroom, and Cina a fragrant piece of honeycomb.

Now, Watka looks deep into Kela's face as if trying to read her thoughts. "Good child, what brings you to me? Is it to do with Omu? Is there any news? I have long since seen what hangs around your neck. My eyes are old, but my sight is still sharp. Kela, this is the greatest gift you can give our people."

Kela respectfully and silently removes the engraved spearhead and hands it to the old woman. Once again, she describes what happened to the falling water. The old woman kisses the spearhead, turns it around, and runs her finger sensitively over the engraving. After a moment of silence, she tenderly takes Kela's hand.

"It's a breach of our law. You all know it. No outsider is allowed to enter our valley. But I believe you, Kela, that the two bobos bring good and pose no danger. We want to bring them into our secret primeval valley and see if they can show us a path that leads to Omu."

Then, Watka's handshake tightens, and her face darkens. "But if they're lying, they won't leave our valley alive."

33

Kela returned to the entrance cave with two strong hunters armed with lances. The bodyguards, wearing bluish make-up and adorned with blue feathers, remained in the background, hardly appearing threatening regardless of how capable they might be of defending themselves. Once again, Kela demonstrated how to roll sideways through the narrow rock window; she led them down the rocky path into the evergreen primeval valley.

"Please pinch me. Is this a dream?" Lilly was on the verge of tears. "Please don't let me wake up now!"

Walker grabbed her hand. "You won't; I'm in the same dream with you. All this is real, a world from another time."

It was immediately apparent that the fairytale-like sinkhole, sealed off from the outside world, provided shelter for a world of flora and fauna unusual in North America today. Its unique climate influenced all forms of life. Completely isolated, this paradisiacal area was home to particularly colorful insect species and a large variety of birds. Oversized, shimmering purple dragonflies buzzed over a wetland the size of a soccer field, lined with old blue oaks and horse chestnuts, a breeding ground for ducks and other waterfowl. Tall cinnamon and devil's ferns stood at the side of the paths. Clinging to the pink blossom of a magnolia, a yellow praying mantis ate a white hummingbird from its clutches. Prairie plums and papaws grew in bright green meadows, and every embankment was covered in a different sea of flowers.

For the biologist in Lilly, there was nothing more exciting than immersing herself in this isolated biosphere, a miniature world with an incomparable animal and plant kingdom. "I read about the Heavenly Pit in Guangxi, a huge sinkhole recently explored by Chinese researchers. But this one is much more impressive, almost legendary."

"It seems to me that some of this plant life is prehistoric," explained Walker. "Some of the lichens, mosses, and ferns I only know from textbooks. I am convinced species have survived in this Eldorado that are otherwise only found in the drawers of natural history museums."

News of the visit spread through the valley like wildfire. As they passed the caves of the hunter-gatherers, a group of brightly painted children in scanty Stone Age clothing ran cheerfully alongside them. The adults did not approach but eyed the strangers suspiciously from a distance. Regardless of the reactions they received, however, the two knew they had no choice but to submit and let themselves be led along the paths.

Crossing the grounds, Lilly was amazed at the state of the ecosystem, which seemed to be completely intact. The inhabitants knew how to preserve and protect their Garden of Eden in all its splendor.

"They live in absolute harmony with nature," she noted. "They probably only hunt and gather outside the valley, and even inside, they only use a small part for their existence; no one tramples through the area, and they always stay on the paths. Look, they mainly stay in the caves!"

The Neanderthals lived in numerous, deeply branched cavities at the foot of the ring of steep slopes. They rested in them, found shelter from heat and stormy weather, and made and stored their products. Some of the caves appeared to have been scraped out with tools. Walker spontaneously thought of the phenomenal passages carved by American giant sloths with their mighty claws in the Pleistocene. The elephant-sized herbivores became extinct around eleven thousand years ago. Did they have access to this valley via a connected tunnel system?

Scarlet, golden yellow and brilliant blue climbing shrubs grew around the cave entrances as if gardeners had planted them. Not a single clan member was to be seen in the central forest area with its immense tree population. The Neanderthals did not enter their forest as if it were the law; they left it alone and avoided its destruction. Exotic animal calls echoed from the thicket, the retreat of a mysterious diversity of species.

They moved deeper and deeper into the karst sinkhole's terrain. The air was still, muggy, and warm; cool clouds of mist lingered in shady hollows. They quenched their thirst at the sparkling stream's natural course, which rippled peacefully through the landscape.

"Pretty big for a beaver!" Lilly pointed to a gigantic rodent on the bank. "It's like a black bear."

"Castoroides!" exclaimed Walker excitedly. "A giant beaver. Animals have *survived* in this place, Lilly, animals of the Ice Age!"

Not far from them, young Neanderthals played wild water games while herons and Clark's grebes searched for food in the distance. Two pelicans hovered majestically above their heads; wild boar, rabbits, partridges, and deer ran around here and there. Lilly thought she could even make out two young Beringian wolves somewhere deep inside the shrubbery. Nowhere did she see garbage, litter or any environmental degradation. The Neanderthals were well aware of the value of their oasis and treated it accordingly.

Walker suspected that the natural waterways served as a sewage treatment plant. Fed by the waterfall, supplies from the outer lake flowed in through fissures, ran on as a stream, and arrived in the branched underground canal system somewhere on the other side. The locals knew the waterways inside out, and what to do during heavy rainfall to avoid being washed away. The use of the specific geographical features of the sinkhole was necessary to hide permanently. Walker was reminded of the discovery of the partial skeleton of an early human adult in 2015 at the entrance to the Mandarin cave in southern France. Its discoverers had named it Thorin after the character from *The Lord of the Rings*. Nine years later, in 2024, a new genetic analysis revealed that Thorin's fossilized bones contain genetic evidence of a Neanderthal lineage that evolved in complete isolation from other European Neanderthals for around fifty thousand years. He knew the survival of a single clan of early humans over a long period of time was possible.

Lilly and Walker followed the two hunters, surrounded by a cloud of sweat odor so intense that it seemed almost visible.

"This is a field test ten times over," Walker said fervently. "All our hard-won scientific knowledge is coming together for me now. It's real, Lilly. I feel like a blind man who can see for the first time!"

He was struck by the realization that these, likely the last of their kind, had also settled into a sedentary life. They had managed to overcome two major challenges: their population remained manageable, and they did not over-hunt the ecosystem where they lived.

New studies show that the extinction of species caused by hominids is not an exclusively modern phenomenon. Around one and a half million years ago, our human ancestors and relatives began to hunt the largest animal available on their hunting grounds, continuing until its species was wiped out. Then, they moved on to the next largest animal and hunted it down in the same way. In the past one hundred and thirty thousand years alone, over two hundred large mammal species and countless birds, marsupials and other animal species have disappeared in this way. However, this clan of modern early humans had presumably learned from its mistakes.

A small group of yellow-faced craftsmen dragged tied-up piles of furs and two hunted wapitis to another party for processing.

"Do you see that? They have separated themselves from their nomadic existence like almost all of humanity's cultures today. That'll be how they found a way to survive in this place for centuries, maybe even millennia."

Lilly nodded. "In such a limited habitat, this is only possible with strict rules. If they had polluted and trampled the ecosystem and destroyed its balance, it would have meant their demise. They have survived because they respect their hidden habitat and avoid exploiting the natural resources."

"Lilly, I think they're smarter than us."

"You don't say! They're showing us how it's done. But even if this jewel may be incredibly informative for mankind... it must not become a sensation!"

34

The fast-paced walk led them into the heart of the area to a slightly elevated, semi-shaded clearing covered in grass, mosses, and orchids. A grove of resinous, fragrant silver firs and sugar pines surrounded the hill. What Walker initially thought were scattered, man-sized boulders were, on closer inspection, actually the dome-shaped back shells of glyptodons, a species of rhinoceros-sized mammal thought to be long extinct.

"Every discovery excites me even more than the last."

"They're spoiling us!" Lilly agreed.

At the hill's center rose an imposing stone circle of twelve monoliths, encircling a vast horseshoe-shaped hearth, long cooled, which Walker judged to span nearly twenty feet across. At its edge, awaiting them, sat Old Watka with a magnificent, gleaming buffalo horn on her broad lap. Kela gently pushed the two visitors toward her; they greeted the elder with a somewhat awkward Buddhist wai greeting and dutifully said their names. When they looked around seconds later, their three companions had vanished from the face of the earth.

Lilly got goosebumps. "That's magical. How did they do that?"

"We can dissolve into nature," Watka replied as if it were the most normal thing in the world. Tilting her head, she looked at the astonished faces before her. "We blend into it because we are a *part* of it, just as you once were. But that was a long time ago. You foolish creatures have lost the most important thing: your connection to Mother Nature. You have long since cut yourselves off from her. That's why we seem *magical*, as you say."

They hadn't expected a Neanderthal woman who spoke their language at all, much less one who did so with such eloquence. Lilly sank onto a stone opposite her. Exhausted and stunned, she shook her head. Walker sat down next to her.

"Who taught you our language?" he asked the old woman.

"Let me tell you the story. I was just six years old when I wandered too far away from the other gatherers here in the mountains. I wandered around, and Salish discovered me. They saw the shape of my head and thought I belonged to one of the Indian tribes in the area. I didn't understand their words and I couldn't defend myself against them, so they took me with them."

"My father told me about the Salish Indians in the Bitterroot Mountains," Lilly recalled. "He said they wrapped their babies' skulls to make them elongated."

"That's right." The woman took a long look at Lilly's youthful, radiant face. "It's an expression of their pride and tribal affiliation. I stayed with them for six summers. They taught me their language... and yours too, I suppose. A white man in a black robe who lived among them spoke it very well. He described himself as a Jesuit, a Catholic priest who wanted to teach the Indian tribes generosity, community, obedience and respect for the family. That's how I learned to talk like you."

Lilly and Walker listened, rapt.

"Over time, however, I became a stranger to the Salish because my nature was increasingly different from theirs. When I was little, we looked alike, but as I grew up and my body matured, they saw me as a stranger, and I stood out as one. So, one night, I left them. All alone in the mountains, I remembered my roots and I found myself able to gather food enough to survive. But I couldn't find my way back to my home, the primeval valley."

Watka opened her fist. In her palm lay the finely engraved spearhead that Kela had given her. Like a blind person who can read through touch, she stroked it gently. "This helped me. One night, deep in the wilderness, I encountered our sacred spearhead in a dream. Lost in the mountains, I saw its engraved symbols in my mind's eye and managed to scratch them into the clay in the moonlight. And so, I remembered, looked for the three giant larches, and found my way back to my people. Of course, I brought some Salish knowledge home with me, which is still useful to my brothers and sisters to this day. They respect me for it and call me *Watka*, The Returned."

"That's an amazing story," Walker marveled. "I know of the Salish and other peoples of the world who bandaged the heads of their children— Maya, Inca, Mangbetu. We once assumed that your people did the same. However, we know now that you are born with this skull shape."

"Do your people, whom we call *bobo*, know about us?" asked the old woman.

Lilly stifled a laugh because '*bobo*' means 'fool' in Spanish—a detail both funny and telling.

"We know a lot about you," Walker confirmed. "But we believe that you have been extinct for a long time, you might be relieved to know. In any case, I am happy to see that this is not the case. You are alive!"

Watka stroked the engraving lovingly. "And you are only alive because you had our relic with you. We are grateful to you and trust you. How did you come to possess it?"

"From a wolf."

The old woman tilted her bulging head far forward, looking inquiringly as Lilly pointed to her own neck vertebrae.

"The tip was stuck in a dead wolf. In the neck. In this exact spot."

"Then, he chased the wolf."

"Who chased him?" asked Lilly.

"Omu," Watka replied. "Our new leader. He is now where the wolf is. He wants to get the spearhead back."

All of a sudden, Lilly understood. Everything made sense. Kela had depicted it in her pantomime: the lover she spoke of, Omu, was chasing after the Beringian wolf. In her mind's eye, she saw the dead animal lying in the small, cold room. She thought of Fred and Tom. *Are they in danger? Could Omu really stalk the wolf over this distance?* She didn't want to believe her thoughts.

"No human can track a wolf for days," she said defiantly.

"It's Omu," Watka replied in a firm voice. "He has the heart of a Kodiak. He is at home on the hunt. He talks to the forest and reads the trail. The wolf does not lie. The animal is injured and weakened, and it betrays itself. Every sound, every scent, every movement, every natural clue is communicated to the hunter. It is probably also mentally connected to him. Omu will, I promise you, chase him to the end."

Walker was thinking of the small San in southern Africa, who can chase much larger and faster prey to death barefoot. As the bushmen sweat through their skin, their wiry bodies are effectively cooled. To quench their thirst, they drink water from filled ostrich eggs and chew on the cactus-like hoodia plant, which keeps them fit and suppresses hunger pangs. With such techniques, the tiny hunters of the Kalahari have an advantage over the fleeing prey.

As far as the Neanderthals' visual abilities were concerned, Walker had on many occasions analyzed skulls and found that their brains had vast regions for visual processing, a clear advantage when hunting. Their keen senses and precise perceptions were likely to greatly benefit them when hunting, not to mention their almost paranormal talents, which cannot be explained by current scientific knowledge. Did they have a sixth sense like some dolphins, which sense the finest electrical fields in the water and use them to track down hidden prey, or like birds that get their bearings from the Earth's magnetic field? Whether paranormal or otherwise, they possessed a certain something that modern man was no longer capable of.

"Is Omu dangerous?" he asked freely, considering the term apex predator.

"Yes, if he wants to be," the old woman replied calmly. "We are a peaceful people, but he is looking for the spearhead and will do anything to get his hands on it. Anyone who tries to stop him in the woods has already lost. Out there, no one can compete with him."

Lilly and Walker exchanged meaningful glances. They had to get back immediately. But an arduous return journey lay ahead, and hunger gnawed at them.

As if the old gatherer could read their thoughts, she said: "Night is already casting its shadows. Stay here by the fire, eat with us and rest until morning. Gather strength for your return! You brought the symbol of our existence back to us. We are eternally grateful for that. Our sacred spear broke in two. Tonight is the night of reunification. A new spear will be erected.

We will celebrate like you have never seen before. Everyone will come, everyone except my old brother Meru. He will stay near the entrance to guard it. That was his will."

35

Frank Stolin knew that he wasn't a particularly respected man. But what did he care? Every man for himself, he thought.

His first wife was a petite hairdresser from the small town of Pocatello in southern Idaho. Yet, he long concealed from her his long-standing relationship with an Indigenous woman who belonged to the Shoshone-Bannock tribe and came from the neighbouring Fort Hall reservation. Her name was Aponi, an Indian word for butterfly. The infidelity was discovered and led to a divorce, and from then on, Stolin no longer received free haircuts.

Two months later, he met an official over a glass of beer at the Juniper Hills Country Club. The man got him a special brokerage job for the Pocatello city council, which wanted to sell a plot of land near the airport to an investor. He succeeded in closing the deal, but the contract was revoked after the courts deemed it to be illegal without the consent of the indigenous tribes. As it later turned out, Frank Stolin had knowingly disregarded the Shoshone-Bannock's right to have a say, even though his partner, Aponi, had pleaded with him. As a result, he lost his position with the city, Aponi the butterfly flew away, and Stolin was single again.

In a way, it suited him to be alone. He appreciated the freedom and a self-determined life. As he was a good shot and could ride a horse to some extent, Painted Rocks State Park hired him as a seasonal game-keeper. He was primarily interested in the steady income and never really took his professional duties seriously, shirking them whenever possible. As soon as an opportunity presented itself, he took his gear out of hiding and pursued his true hobbies: hunting and trapping.

It wasn't just the extra income he earned from his leisure activity that appealed to him; trapping and killing wild animals brought him deep satisfaction and gave him back much-needed self-confidence. He proved his absolute supremacy over the animals with every pelt he captured. Heavily armed, he was vastly superior to them in the merciless wilderness.

Be fruitful, and multiply, and replenish the earth, and subdue it: and have dominion over the fish of the sea, and over the fowl of the air, and over every living thing that moveth upon the earth. (Genesis 1:28 King James Version)

Stolin understood the words of the Bible to be a clear authorization from God, one that no earthly law could change. He firmly believed that all life in the wild had to be unconditionally subordinate to man and his needs. Stolin was no conscientious hunter, and in reality he misunderstood the true meaning of this verse. He never considered that every exercise of power brings with it a high degree of responsibility.

Hunting and trapping remain deeply ingrained in American culture. Yet the extermination of fur-bearing species, as happened two centuries ago, must never be repeated. State authorities regulate which animals may be hunted, when, and where—balancing economics, game populations, habitat, and safety—while still facing the relentless demand of millions of hunters, whose hunger is great and whose greed greater.

Stolin knew that he could legally hunt a number of animal species on land open to the public with the necessary license. However, if he occasionally found a protected specimen in the trap or front of the barrel of his rifle and no one was looking, he always remembered those lines of scripture and pulled the trigger mercilessly.

The government currently classifies thirteen thousand North American animal species as endangered; for Stolin, this large number was a scandal, an excessive patronization of free and proud Americans.

In his greed for trophies, his defiance led him to make no distinction between hunting and poaching. When he grew bored of deer, waterfowl, turkeys and wild boar, he would occasionally treat himself to a challenging big game hunt in Alaska, where he enthusiastically caught and killed bison, caribou, moose, musk oxen, wolves, Dall sheep, Sitka black-tailed deer, mountain goats and black, brown and grizzly bears. With such 'high-quality' hunting, as he used to put it at local pub meetups, he could 'harvest' game protected in other states' more strictly regulated areas.

Sometimes, hunting was frustrating for him. If a coyote had bitten off its foot in a foot trap, causing Stolin to miss out on well-deserved, albeit meager, income, he would, for his edification, recall the history of those trappers who had played such a glorious role in the colonization of North America and who had bravely ventured into unknown Indian territories with their rifles and explored them for subsequent settlers.

Many of these first trappers had several wives, one in each Native American tribe, be it Hidatsa, Shoshone, or Crow. He thought his former girlfriend, Aponi, gave his resume a special historical glow. She helped him stand out honorably from the legion of one hundred thousand American trappers active today, who capture over five million furs a year.

But the greatest inner strength for Frank Stolin came from his Ruger American Rifle. A life without his faithful companion seemed unimaginable to him. Even today, his rifle protected him as he sat around waiting alone all day while the lovebirds from Salt Lake City ran completely unarmed to their doom. He thought that indeed served them right; after all, he had warned them about this hellmouth.

It was hot, but he didn't give the horses a drop of water, hoarding it for himself. *Just in case*, he thought. The eerie voices at the waterfall were still buzzing around in his head. There was something wrong with the place, just as something was wrong with the two adventurers. *Are they injured? In trouble? They should have been back long ago! Well, it's their fault and God's punishment if anything happened to them.*

But that didn't mean he was off the hook as a gamekeeper. Trouble was in the air. What was he supposed to do if the two didn't return? A missing person's report under his guidance meant nothing but trouble and would further damage his reputation. Apart from that, he would have to make the ride back through the mountains alone, which he distrusted. It was much safer with others.

Wrestling with himself and his fear, he nervously played with the bolt of his rifle, thinking hard about what to do. Perhaps they were doing even better than he thought. Maybe they were secretly looking for something valuable. Had they just used him as a guide and conspired against him? In that case, it was better to follow the two secretive people to determine what they were up to.

It was already getting dark. Tomorrow morning, then!

36

Watka straightened up, held the horn to her mouth, took a deep breath and blew so hard that her bright blue cheeks puffed out like the vocal sac of a frog. With lips drawn taut, she blew into the curved horn, sending a column of air vibrating into a deep, majestic sound. The signal reached every corner of the primeval valley, echoed in the bushes, penetrated the narrowest cave passages, rebounded on the angular rocks of the cliffs and was reflected from them thousands of times.

Soon, the first of the clan appeared: old, young, red, yellow, and blue, some with flower and feather decorations and others in full hunting gear. They brought with them countless leather bags, baskets and wooden vessels filled with fish, tubers, mushrooms, forest fruits, herbs, and nuts; dragged along six young boars, two dozen forest rabbits and four roebucks; and transported neatly tied stacks of firewood and all the extras.

Lilly and Walker watched with interest as the turbulent events gradually developed into an unprecedented barbecue. No one gave instructions; there was no hierarchy. But it worked. Everyone had their task and worked toward the common goal.

By now, there must have been around two hundred Neanderthals. In no time, some were skinning and cutting up the prey with their razor-sharp stone tools. Others built fires and used simple tools to press bark into the hearth, slowly rendering it into sticky birch tar. Cooks mixed spices and fat into pastes in wooden bowls, artfully speared fish on bony hooks, and filled woven containers with ripe wild fruits.

As dusk fell, torches were lit on the twelve monoliths of the stone circle, and furs were spread out around them. Children ran around happily, playing hide-and seek in hollow glyptodon shells, and teenagers joined each other by chattering, setting fire to grass balls, and scuffling playfully in the dirt. Experienced hunters proudly showed off their finest weapons.

"A shared campfire," Walker enthused, "is magical. It's like a spell from ancient times; it puts us in a trance... it changes the way we experience the world, how we see and hear, how our brains work... how we perceive others."

"I perceive you with pleasure, Walker," Lilly said, resting her head on his shoulder.

The meal began. The tribe members kept a respectful distance from Lilly and Walker. Watka had disappeared. Only Kela remained close to them. She handed them game stewed on a stone, bowls full of fragrant mushrooms, fruit balls kneaded with flowers and honey, and fresh drinking water. It was all delicious. They politely declined only the fresh offal.

Walker cut up an oversized piece of wild boar leg with his K4 Leatherman. He saw that Kela was fascinated by the stainless-steel folding knife, so he lent it to her. She repeatedly folded and unfolded every tool, from the spring scissors to the awl. She had never touched such a shiny, rigid and yet flexible material. As the folding knife was indispensable to Walker, he kindly asked her to return it. In return, he passed over his Akubra, which barely fit the lumpy head of the little Stone Age woman. Kela thanked him by rubbing her broad nose tenderly against his knee and massaging his calf. Walker rolled his eyes and pulled himself together to keep from laughing.

Neanderthals could devour vast quantities of raw meat and roasted seasoned pieces. Their mouth and teeth would stop at nothing, crushing entire carcasses, eating large fish heads, biting through the ribs of piglets and gnawing at the bones until the marrow was exposed. They rubbed their oily hands over parts of their bodies that were unclothed as if they were anointing themselves.

Lilly watched as a group of breastfeeding and pregnant women squatted together and chatted animatedly, as a circle of old women and men brought children bowls of soup and as lovers rubbed their fat noses together. Behind the monoliths of the stone circle, small wrestling matches were taking place between youths. It was not uncommon for their robust skulls to collide and sound like bowling balls hitting the lane. The fighters were powerful and lightning-fast but also showed mutual fairness and respect. Walker admitted that some looked a lot more fearsome than the replicas in the Neanderthal Museum near Düsseldorf.

The smoke from the feast rose in the sinkhole and evaporated into the starry night sky. *No barbecue in the world could compete with this,* thought Walker, and he had experienced more than a few in his life. In terms of taste, it was a real treat for him. Lilly was amused that his face was no less smeared than the Neanderthals'. She wasn't a big meat eater but was no less indulgent with the stewed delicacies that evening.

"A condiment mix of the finest quality," Walker judged and burped loudly. "Do you have any idea which supermarket they got it from?"

Lilly laughed and joked: "Just imagine the look on the cashier's face!"

"It tastes like it has salt in it. But where do you get it in an area like this?"

"Good question, my dear. As a doctor, I can tell you that they also *need* a salt supply. Maybe they burn dry coltsfoot leaves. The ash is rich in salt. But my guess is pecan root. Something like that thrives here in the valley. My father showed it to me a few years ago. On a trip to the Rocky Mountains, he fired up our little gas stove and boiled down pieces of pecan root. What remained was a salty mineral extract. We used it to season our meat."

Suddenly, there was silence. At an inaudible command, everyone stopped what they were doing. No one continued eating, no one moved, no one spoke. Then, after a few minutes, a peculiar murmur went through the crowd. All eyes turned to three approaching figures adorned in red, yellow, and blue. They were the splendidly dressed elders. The crowd had made way as they moved to the center of the clearing.

Crowned with stuffed wolf heads that towered over their heads, they walked slowly and meaningfully forward, moving one by one along the clearing into the middle of the stone circle toward the large horse-shoe-shaped hearth, which was open at one point. They held up ceremonial objects with both hands and kept turning round and round. It looked strange and different from any Native American ceremony Lilly had ever witnessed. Walker was just as fascinated as she was.

Hani, the eldest of the red tribe of producers, walked ahead. He carried a stone vessel filled with hot birch tar, whose steaming vapors rose into the sky in rings as he rotated. Taku, the leader of the yellow tribe of craftsmen, followed him. As he turned, Taku proudly showed off his hunting knife made of deer antlers and carved flint. He held a bundle of animal sinew wound into a ring in his other hand. Finally, Old Watka towered over everyone with a carefully sharpened wooden shaft that was six and a half feet long, which Walker thought was the prepared blank of the new spear.

The palaeoanthropologist was close enough to recognize that the shape of the shaft resembled the Schöningen spears, the world's oldest fully preserved hunting weapons. They were found in an open-cast lignite mine in Germany at the end of the 1990s and date back to the Palaeolithic period. The maker of these spears was Homo heidelbergensis, an ancestor of Neanderthal man. Three hundred thousand years ago, he was already grinding long, straight stems from suitable spruce wood so that the largest diameter and center of gravity were in the front third of the shaft. The javelins had to be just the right length and weight.

Woodworking involves cutting and stripping the bark, carving it into an aerodynamic shape, scraping off a large part of the surface, seasoning the wood to prevent cracks and deformation, and carefully shaping the tips.

In field trials, replicas of the Schöningen spears proved to be on par with spears used in competition today, flying over two hundred and thirty feet and likely being lethal to big game at sixty-five feet. The makers knew the inner pith of a shaft was softer than the outer wood, so they shaped the spear's ends off-center, away from the core, to give it greater strength. However, the shaft that Watka carried in front of her had no sharpened end. As with the lost spear, it was fitted with a socket.

Now, Lilly saw the small but beautiful object that everything revolved around: in the open mouth of the wolf's skull above the old gatherer was the engraved spearhead, surrounded by fearsome fangs. Crackling with heat, the shimmering embers turned Watka's sweating skin purple-red as the three circled closer to the hot center. The audience passionately joined the distorted rhythmic screams and entered a frenzy. *Are hallucinogenic mushrooms or an occult herbal mixture having an effect?* Lilly wonders. *Or did the constant twirling of the leaders alone send the whole clan into ecstasy?*

The ceremony took on an increasingly daring character. Keeping their balance on the last narrow footbridge to where the fire was to avoid stumbling into the embers demanded a high degree of body control. Lilly feared that a slight misstep would cost one of them their lives.

The sight of it made Walker dizzy, too. He tried to maintain a clear head, analyzing what was happening, assuming that the strange maneuver was both a ritual and a test of courage. Numerous members of the tribe were spinning around like dancing drunks, indulging in intoxication while making bizarre noises. Without the Australian realizing it, he became part of the whole thing and howled at the top of his lungs. Lilly looked at him in amazement until she realized she was howling, too.

Arriving at the center of the vast glowing ring of fire, Watka rammed the wooden shaft vertically into the ground. Then, with both hands, she reached into the mouth of her headdress, fingers searching until they found the spearhead. She drew it out slowly, lifted it high toward the star-filled sky, and let out a fervent cry—the crowd answering with a roar. She spoke words that seemed significant, which Lilly and Walker did not understand, but the whole crowd cheered.

The three tribal leaders now worked together to join the tip of the projectile to the shaft. Drenched in sweat, Watka inserted the magnificent barbed spearhead into the cone-shaped socket. Hani served Taku with animal sinew and birch tar. While the three moved steadily around the wooden shaft, clearly visible to all, Taku, the oldest of the craftsmen, skillfully tied the engraved bone head, tightened the loops and carefully glued all the parts together to form a whole.

The spear was back in the center of the clan, and unity was restored. For a long time, the five tribes danced jubilantly around their renewed sanctuary.

Before dawn, they extinguished the fire's embers and fell asleep, snorting peacefully, scattered by the hundreds across the clearing.

37

Stolin hadn't slept a wink all night. The long wait was wearing him out. What's more, his water supply was running low, and—search as he might—none of his pockets contained any whiskey. Tired and disgruntled, he dug a long strip of jerky from Lilly's bag, shoved it in his mouth and washed it down with a big gulp from the thermos flask. He shouldn't have done that. Instead of chewing it leisurely, the tough, unsoftened meat was sent agonizingly down his throat until the trapper was in tears from the pain.

"What the hell am I waitin' here for anyway?" he cursed into the wilderness.

For him, the whole project was a farce. They wouldn't find the Beringian wolf, and all the while he was losing out on his usual profits. He grew more furious thinking of how the lucrative prey caught in his traps would already be rotting. Given all these circumstances, he concluded that there was probably nothing left to do but pursue the Salt Lake City lovers, not least because he couldn't muster the courage to return alone.

"Enough already! Whatever you're doin', I'm going to get you," he declared, shooting up from the rock on which he had perched.

"I've got my gun, and I'm not afraid of nothin'."

He carelessly tied the horses, grumpily stuffed two boxes of cartridges into his pockets, threw the rifle sling over his shoulder and set off a second time along the narrow path to the mountain lake.

On the way, the ghostly voices seemed to return. He felt uneasy, not having any idea of what awaited him this time. He tried to think clearly. What he heard by the lake, he told himself, was simply the echo of an animal call, or maybe just the wind whistling through the cliffs. Ghosts didn't exist in real life. Or did they?

As he saw it, there were only three possible scenarios: the lovers were either in serious trouble, betraying him, or pursuing their physical desires. If they were in trouble, he would decide on the spur of the moment what to do. At best, he would save them and ensure it gave his reputation an overdue makeover. Perhaps there would be bloodshed, but he was well-armed, which gave him power. Compassion was fortunately not one of his weaknesses.

He would react very differently if it turned out that they were, in fact, deceiving him, gaining some kind of advantage, and ostracizing him in the process. As a child, he often lost his temper and seriously hurt others in instances where he was disadvantaged. The resulting punishments had in no way caused him to show remorse. On the contrary, they hardened his will to look out for himself.

Finally, the third scenario seemed the most likely. He had only imagined the voices—he'd experienced his fair share of whiskey-induced hallucinations before now. And so, it seemed probable to him that he would catch the lovers taking a lewd dip in the lake, watch them from a concealed vantage point for a while, and then make them perform in a way they had never experienced before.

After he had passed the last bend, the lake lay calm in front of him. Only the waterfall threw ripples over its glittering surface. Still, the beauty of the kingdom was lost on him. Even worse, there was no sign of the lovers. A steady roar suddenly echoed from all sides of the rock mass. Swaths of fine spray wafted through the oppressively warm morning air. The trapper stood frozen in place for several minutes, fleet-footed and ready to shoot. Yet he heard no ghostly voices and saw nobody dead or alive in the water or on land.

Searching, he walked and climbed all the accessible parts of the sinkhole as far as he could reach, looked around puzzled, but found no niches, tunnels or climbing walls. On closer inspection, only the water-fall remained. Stolin walked up close to it. He couldn't see through it. He was reluctant to get wet. But he had no choice if he didn't want to rack his brains for the rest of his life, wondering if something was behind it. He had to do it.

"Damn it!"

He took a deep breath, squeezed his eyes shut, took three fumbling steps forward, then a fourth, and found himself standing on dry ground, water dripping from him. He had entered the shadowland.

"Uh-huh!"

He opened his eyes abruptly. The bright light of the narrow rock opening shone into the gloomy grotto like a spotlight. He immediately loaded his hunting rifle and strode toward it. No longer could he suppress the idea that the two out-of-towners were intentionally hiding from him. He carefully positioned himself at the edge of the passage, avoiding quick movements so as not to be spotted, and scanned the panorama of the primeval valley with the skilled eye of a hunter.

He was not interested in the geological formation of the Elysian basin or the peacefully grazing black and red deer that presented themselves for the kill. Transporting prey from here would be too difficult anyway. Instead, Stolin sought two-legged friends: the wolf expert and her Australian ally.

He suddenly noticed a human figure. About five hundred feet away, it was crouching alone in one of the many caves that lined the steep walls. Which of the traitors it was, he did not know. He couldn't see enough with the naked eye, but he knew that the rifle scope on his Ruger would help.

Stolin got into position. He dropped to one knee on the cold stone, eased the loaded rifle into the rock's notch with the utmost care, then peered through the eyepiece and cranked the scope to its highest magnification. The threefold magnification of the daytime lens enabled him to see more details. To his surprise, though, it was neither Feron nor Walker who was crouching there.

The gruesome stories told by fellow trappers and hunters at the tavern immediately came to mind—tales of monstrous, savage clans that tied the skulls of their children to disfigure them. Stolin had done some research, and it was true. These godforsaken sadists had been wreaking havoc in the Bitterroot Mountains since the eighteenth century. It was obvious to him that they had something to do with the disappearance of peaceful hikers in the region. If they were still roaming around here, they were a danger.

That savage down there... indeed, he was one of them! The blue-painted face, the bulbous and elongated skull shape—Stolin had little doubt that it was one of the deformed monsters he'd heard about. If even the slightest bit of aggressive behavior toward him, an American gamekeeper, it was his legitimate duty to defend himself by any means necessary and then report the case to the authorities.

But then something unexpected happened. As if some thought had leapt between them, the figure suddenly turned and fixed its gaze on him. A cold shiver ran down Stolin's spine, and he felt a tingling from somewhere within his heart. Undeterred by his presence, the creature straightened up stolidly and moved straight toward him, all the while keeping its eyes fixed on his with an almost hypnotic gaze.

The trapper tore himself away with force, looked aside, took two steps back into the cave and collected himself. He remembered his Bible verse, hunting rifle, and decades of marksman experience. *Come on, man! You gotta show 'em what a real American looks like*, he told himself. Over the years, numerous fearless game had approached him head-on, running toward him brashly or defending their young. He knew from experience that he had to remain calm, perform well, and avoid the slightest mistake. *This is your big test, Franky boy.*

The danger was approaching; the decisive moment had arrived. He reacted automatically and emotionlessly. He began by closing his eyes briefly, relaxing, feeling the ground and letting it carry him. Then, he tilted his upper body forward and turned slightly to the left until he only touched the stone with the right side of his chest. This way, his heartbeat did not irritate him, nor let him know of his own increasing fear.

The figure was several feet closer by now.

Stolin laid his left hand flat, avoiding pressing on the optics, barrel, or bolt so as not to change the point of impact. With his elbows securely braced, he drew the butt of the rifle into his shoulder without tensing up. His shooting vest would reduce the recoil. He released the safety catch and aimed, selecting the chest area of the approaching creature, now two hundred feet away.

The shooter reduced his breathing. He concentrated, allowing his bent index finger to brush lightly against the trigger. He exhaled calmly. Slowly increased the pressure on the trigger. Paused for breath. And released.

The bullet pierced old Meru's ribcage even before he could hear the sound waves of the muzzle blast. Fatally hit, Watka's brother slumped backward.

38

A little after morning had broken above ground, daylight penetrated deep into the lushly overgrown hollow. In search of food scraps, a family of raccoons made their way through the crowd of Neanderthals scattered across the clearing, sleeping off the night's tremendous feast.

In Lilly's dream, the wild revelry had continued in the rooms of her wolf park. Hordes of prehistoric humans lay on the cupboards, under the tables, next to the chairs, even in the bathtub. One sprawled across the operating table. Greasy barbecued meat was piled up several feet high on the couch, and a sparking campfire was burning in the kitchen.

"Enough!" Lilly screamed in panic. But Walker came to her rescue, appearing at her side in the way that lovers do in dreamland. He held a flare gun and shouted: *"Go home now! The party's over."* Then, he shot into the ceiling, and Lilly woke up.

It was only a dream, but the shot was real. It still echoed from one side of the sinkhole to the other. It took her a while to come to. She pulled herself together and looked around to notice a great unrest among the Neanderthals.

Walker was already on his feet and offered his hand. "Come quickly!" he shouted vehemently. "That could only have been Stolin." "Oh God!" cried Lilly in horror.

They saw Kela dashing down the path like a marten. They hastily grabbed their bags. Just as they were about to join the horde streaming down to the valley entrance, Watka approached them.

"My brother! I can feel his last breath. Come with us, the elders!" she ordered sternly. "That way, you'll be safe from your people and mine."

39

From his shooting position, the trapper continued to aim the rifle scope at the fallen man. He kept him stoically in his sights, examining his bloody chest in the crosshairs to make sure he wasn't moving. *Oh boy, now this is true hunting,* he told himself. *Nobody's ever gonna dare question you again, Frank.*

For another thirty seconds, the echoes of the shot whipped from one cliff face to the next. The shooter inspected the area one last time, then crawled through the passage and made his way down the gravel path into the valley. Repeatedly, he sought cover behind rocky outcrops and bushes at the side of the path to avoid being seen by whatever other beasts may live in the place he had discovered.

Having reached the foot of the towering rock mass, he could get a close-up glimpse into the foremost, lightless grottoes. He realized that they appeared to be inhabited but were currently deserted. He wanted and had to go in. His hopes of discovering something valuable were too high.

With his bolt-action rifle loaded, he stalked hesitantly into the first dwellings. To his astonishment, he found the storage facilities of an entire clan. In one cavity, he spotted game meat and other food supplies; in another, heaps of flint and baskets of colorful minerals. Still, there was no gold, silver or precious stones, all of which he would have much preferred.

Smaller niches contained sparsely furnished sleeping quarters. In another cave, five-foot-high heaps of bones, antlers, predator teeth, and skulls made him shudder. He was more convinced than ever that true beasts were vegetating here, and he would do well to get out as possible before they returned to lynch him.

Just as he told himself that nothing would keep him here, however, several piles of furs hoarded in a side wing cast a spell on him. Forgetting everything else, he leaped at them. Surveying their condition, he hurried from one pile to the next, lifting individual layers, running his hand over them, sniffing them, and examining the hides from below. The trapper soon realized the immense value of the find, and burst into a smug, maniacal laughter. As if in a dream, he was presented with the finest furs of rare species, including grizzlies, raccoons, moose, black bears, red wolves, Cozumel raccoons, and bison. It seemed to him that they were waiting for him—waiting to be transported.

40

Kela runs as if stung by a wasp.

After the wonderful ceremony, she slept soundly. In her dream, she ran far into the forest to find Omu a green mushroom. It was supposed to protect him from evil.

Delighted, she saw one of these poisonous mushrooms standing in a small, sunlit clearing. She carefully dug it out of the ground and opened her raffia basket to stow it away. Then, a thunderstorm rolled in. First, a flash of lightning and then a mighty clap of thunder almost ruptured her eardrums.

She woke suddenly. The thunder was still drumming like countless hard rockfalls in the furrows of the surrounding rock faces. She jumped up. The barbecue area was in chaos. Sisters and brothers were running around upset. In the confusion of echoes, she located the direction of the bang. The source was at the entrance to the primeval valley, near the caves of the blue tribe. Horrified, she realized that it was a rifle shot that she had heard in her sleep. She also guessed who it was aimed at, grabbed the bobo man's gifted hat, and stormed off.

Young and nimble, she is among the first to reach the spot. It would take a while for the elders to arrive. Three young, wiry brothers had already arrived at the scene. Kela kneels and lays her forehead on Meru's bloody chest, weeping. He was her father's father. The bullet went right through his heart, and the murderer is gone.

Her people know about the bobo guns from Watka's stories. The weapons are merciless, supernatural, loud, and lightning-fast. They give their prey no chance to react. It is too easy to kill animals and humans with them. They are the weapons of cowardly hunters—killing with their help is a disgrace instead of an honor.

If only Omu were in the valley! Kela thinks about him all the time. But why did she dream about him and the greenling mushroom? This mushroom is one of her people's three poisons: the frog's poison, the mushroom, and the snake.

"Ja-ni, wu-ma, mat-ki," she lists the three poisons in an incantation, and she feels Omu is very close. "May they benefit you in danger!" she sends to him.

The others will soon arrive. Kela is worried about her high-headed friends. If the brothers and sisters of the Primeval Valley find the bullet, they will bring the bobos to justice.

Kela wants to get ahead of it. Like two slow worms, her slender fingers glide skillfully into Meru's open wound, digging deep until they can grasp the hard bullet and pull it out. The bullet is heavy and smeared with vibrant blood. Kela sniffs it, puts it in her mouth, and cleans it until it once again shines like polished hematite. Then, she keeps the deadly bullet in one of the pouches on her clothing. No one should see it.

More brothers and sisters flock around the dead man. A tracker is already following the murderer's trail to the grottoes. A growing crowd gathers there.

"He's in there," shouts one of them. "The intruder is in the burrow; it can't escape."

Kela expects that there will soon be accusations. She is already hearing voices of reproach and accusations that the murderer belongs to the two bobos.

"Let Taku see the deceased!" orders Watka.

"Is the murderer part of your gang?" a sister from the yellow tribe calls out to the bobos, but they don't understand the language of the primeval people.

Kela stands back while Taku inspects the corpse. His fingers dig deep into the flesh, but he finds no bullet.

"*Where is it?*" *he asks.* "*Where's the bullet?*"

Hani looks questioningly at Kela and sees from her expression that she has taken it.

Don't betray me, Kela thinks, pressing her lips together in a silent plea. Hani understood—and says nothing.

Suddenly, one of the wiry hunters points at her and shouts: "*She's got it! She's got the bullet!*"

With Walker's hat on her head, Kela jumps in horror. Meru's blood is still on her lips and forehead. Two blue-faced gatherers immediately grab her arms roughly, but old Hani steps in, and they let her go.

"*Stop that at once!*" *hisses old Watka.*

At this moment, another shot rings out. The muffled bang comes from one of the dark caves. In an instant, a caregiver with green make-up collapses in the middle of the crowd. Blood oozes from her hip. Members of the white tribe immediately attend to her. Another shot is fired, whipping into the yellow face of a workman, who falls to the ground like a stone. The bullet is deadly, lightning-fast, and invisible. The crowd recoils in horror. Four blue-faced hunters swarm out to the flanks of the cave entrance and take cover. One attempts to advance inside, and a fourth shot narrowly misses him.

A loud finger whistle from the shell ornament man attracts everyone's attention. Walker steps out of the crowd, holds up his hands and walks step by step toward the cave entrance. He shouts urgent words to the murderer. Lilly, the yellow-haired bobo woman, also steps forward, speaks soothingly to him and expresses her defenselessness with raised arms.

"*Our human visitors want to talk to him,*" *explains Old Watka calmly.*

"*Let them do it!*"

Kela's heart beats wildly. She is full of hopes and fears. All those present follow her as the two courageously climb into the dark interior and listen to the voices echoing in the light. No one but Watka understands this language, but everyone senses its meaning: the bobos are in the den, trying to tame the intruder.

Nobody can see them, but they can hear them all the better. At first, the conversation sounds calm and friendly. But it becomes louder and sharper until words of resentment hover in the air.

"It's going to end badly," agitated Kela shouts. She wants to go in and help her friends, but Watka holds her back.

"Wait and see!" the old woman orders. "Don't do anything!"

The argument becomes increasingly violent. Suddenly, Kela hears the sounds of a fight, kicks and jumps, a bright scream, and then... a shot. The opponents clash again, punching and moaning, sliding and snorting. Finally, the pain-filled scream of a man is heard, and silence falls.

Four hunters storm into the rocky cave from the flanks. Kela jumps after them as quickly as she can. At first, she barely sees anything in the cave's darkness, but then, the bright figure of the white woman appears. She seems to be all right. Her dark, curly-haired partner is with her, bruised but in good health, with a small wound on his arm.

The long rifle lies on the ground next to the murderer. A knife is stuck in his eye, the flashing knife of the shell ornament man.

41

Fred's phone buzzed him out of a deep sleep. He was lying on the double bed in his boss's bedroom, wondering how he had gotten there. He was even more surprised that Omu was lying next to him.

He took the call. It was Stan. He spoke in a quiet, shaky voice.

"It's the FBI. They're on their way."

"Oh God! To us? On the way here?"

"They got wind of this bonehead. These guys think the spearhead is in Feron Wolf Park."

"Do they know about *him*?" asked Fred.

"Maybe."

"What do I do now?"

"Release him!"

"He already is."

"Excuse me?"

"He's here with me. Slept with me... I mean, slept beside me."

"What?"

"We're friends now. His name is Omu."

"Holy cow!"

Omu woke abruptly, shot up, stood on the mattress, and listened. Now, Fred heard it, too. Vehicles were circling the building. Engines roared; the gravel crunched, and the wolves responded with panicked, desperate howls. The raid unfolded like a movie, happening so fast that any chance of escape was blocked before it even came to mind.

Pale with horror, Fred realized that fear was also written all over Omu's face. He tore himself away from the early man's haunting expression and ran from the office to the kitchen. Omu followed.

Through the wide window, they saw a silver Bronco SUV park near the house's entrance, kicking up dust. Two men in blue jackets stamped with the bold yellow insignia of the FBI slid out, looking around nervously, intimidated by the wolf howls. One of them wore sunglasses, and the other carried a briefcase.

"That's them. Omu, you've got to get out of here!" shouted Fred, staring helplessly at the officers as they moved toward the entrance. "They want this thing, this projectile, and probably you too!"

He turned to Omu, but he was no longer in the kitchen. The front doorbell rang. Fred ran back to the main office. He wasn't there either.

"Omu, where are you? You have to hide! Omu!"

The doorbell rang again. Fred felt compelled to crack the door and trust that Omu was intelligent enough to navigate his own side. Still, his heart was in his mouth.

The agent introduced himself politely: "Jonathan Foul, FBI. We have a few questions for you." He smiled coolly, slid his badge through the gap, and then pushed the door open forcefully with his elbow. The badge read FBI / SPECIAL AGENT.

"My boss isn't here," Fred protested, knowing he couldn't suppress the lingering uncertainty in his voice.

"Never mind that. Can we talk?" asked Foul as he pushed his way in.

They had no intention of waiting for an answer. The two agents were making their way past him. Fred backed away as if stunned, stammering something about "search warrant" and "trespassing," to which neither responded. "Is something wrong?" he asked himself, following them inside the building like a dachshund.

A woman was standing at the crate. She wore a mask, a white overall with a hood, white disposable overboots and blue nitrile chemical protective gloves. She had entered the office via the delivery entrance.

"Who is Omu?" she asked gruffly without introducing herself. She had heard what Fred had shouted to the Neanderthal, who silently cursed his own oversight. "Who is Omu?" she asked again more sharply.

Fred ignored the question. He would never betray his new friend, and certainly not his boss, but he feared the agents would break him down at any moment. He felt dizzy and had to sit down. Of all places, he sank back into the armchair opposite the picture—the same spot where he had dozed off earlier. The agents promptly noticed Omu's drawing and nodded meaningfully to each other.

"This is exactly the object we're looking for," said Foul, pointing to the unmistakable spearhead. "We have reason to believe that it was stolen from a university lab."

"Hey, I'm just an intern, alright? Fred, the intern. That thing's not here."

"Where is it then?"

"I have no idea. I *swear* I've never seen it."

The other agents worked their way through the complex in military style.

"Who painted the picture?" Foul asked again, his tone now highly unpleasant.

"Who is Omu?" the white-masked woman asked him.

"There's a dead wolf back here!" an agent shouted excitedly from the back of the building. "In a cold room."

"This is a wolf enclosure!" Fred defended himself. "A wolf enclosure with a veterinary clinic. There was a wildlife accident. A wolf came under the wheels, you know? My boss is a vet. She brought him to the clinic to be examined. If you're gonna get all flustered by a dead wolf, a wolf clinic really might not be…"

"Sir!" Foul cut him off. "The wolf is meaningless," he yelled back to his colleague in the cold room before turning his attention back to Fred. "Just listen! We're looking for that thing on the wall. It's a hunting tool."

"Why are you so obsessed with it?" asked Fred cheekily, wondering where Omu could be.

"Because it's a unique weapon."

The special agent was visibly irritated at Fred's growing confidence, but tried to control himself. He sat down on the sofa beside the trainee.

"Listen to me! Your boss is the vet, Lilly Feron. We know that."

"So what?"

"*So…* she cut that object out of a dead wolf. Presumably, that wolf is the one back there in your freezer, right?"

"I don't know."

"Then, she sent it to a ranger named Stan Hardy. Do you know *him?* Mr. Hardy sent it to Utah University to a certain Professor Walker. Do you know *him?* In the professor's apartment, we found the empty DHL package and a note with the address of this wolf park. So, you see, we've come full circle. If you lie to us, we'll know."

"Fine, it seems like you know it all then. So what's the problem?" asked Fred defiantly. The more they talked, the more he was in his element.

"It was stolen, boy! That's the problem! Professor Walker had the hunting instrument examined in the university lab. The next day, it disappeared. The lab assistant reported the theft to the police. And Walker had been there that night. We have proof."

"Theft? What do you mean?" asked Fred. "The professor gave it to the lab to examine it. That's what you just said. Then, he took it back. That's allowed. Or do you think he stole it from himself?"

The agents exchanged puzzled glances. The redhead, they realized, was not at all stupid.

"Whose hunting instrument is this anyway?" Fred asked.

"The state's. It belongs to the state," Foul replied angrily as he rose from the sofa. "It's of national interest."

"Doesn't it belong to the person who used it, I mean, the hunter?"

The other agent took off his sunglasses and stood there, squinting at him with bewilderment.

Foul, visibly irritated, came within an inch of Fred. "Then, tell me where that hunter is! I can smell him!"

He could be right about that. Omu's pungent body odor was everywhere. The agents were more interested in Omu than the projectile tip.

"This is a veterinary clinic. And my boss is away for a while. So, there's nobody here, okay? All these people you're mentioning... Lilly and the professor... Stan somebody—none of them are around. So, now, I have to take care of our wolves. Wolves have horrible diseases that can also be transmitted to humans. Didn't you know? After that, everything is transmitted from person to person... You can smell it! That's what I call national interest."

"Shut your mouth, big boy!" The man in sunglasses exploded. "Diseases don't smell!"

They came up against a stubborn trainee, but they were lucky: the woman in protective clothing had found Omu's stone axe at the crate's edge. Before she picked it up, she illuminated it with a small LED lamp and took photos.

"Well, what have we here!" she said with a start. "Another flashy tool! An axe in the style of the Palaeolithic era. Also perfectly made."

Fred could tell that she was familiar with the material. She put the weapon in a plastic bag, waving it triumphantly in Fred's face. "And now, speak up! Whoever makes or uses something like this is certainly not harmless. So... where... is... he...?" she sputtered.

Fred buried his face in his hands. The agents knew, and his confidence had crumbled.

"Search everything!" Foul commanded. "If he's not in the building, look in the forest! Take the search dogs with you! He's fair game now. Use the axe to help the dogs identify the scent. Hold it out to them!" He pointed his finger at Fred. "And *you*, don't move! You're in trouble now, *trainee*."

In the yard, three dog handlers leashed up their Belgian Malinois. The chase would soon begin.

42

The small window, located on the green side of the den, proves to be a useful entrance and exit. Omu slips through headfirst. Lush purple and white hydrangeas grow outside, into which he slides silently. The few bushes are enough for him to conceal himself like a lizard quickly.

The lizard listens and sniffs. The air is clear. They are not here yet. He creeps forward to the edge of the forest, dives into the thicket and disappears silently. Omu is back in his element.

He doesn't want to stray far; he must stay close to the redhead he trusts. Fred became his ally in finding the spearhead. He warned him when he recognized the danger of the arriving bobos. Omu read not only fear in his face but also worry that they would find and seize him. A true brother!

The hunter will hold out in the forest until they are gone. Soon, hopefully, the woman with the sun hair will come and give him what is his. He thinks of his Kela and wants so much to get back to her. Time passes slowly, like a slug. Omu can guess what the bobos, who have just arrived, want. Their voices and the howling of their dogs all sound so menacing. He suspects they are after his life and wants to get their hands on the engraved spearhead.

Never!

He is startled. In his mind's eye, he sees his stone axe. In his haste, he left it behind on the ground. They will find it, use it, and let their dogs pick up his scent and chase him. He senses that the hunt is on for him. They will enter the forest to capture him.

He does not want to fight. Fighting is not in the nature of his people. They know no greed and no war and have no enemies or pursuers. For they are *invisible to the world from which they hide. Every inhabitant of the prime-val valley knows the following words that are as old as stone:*

"Camouflage is superior to combat because what does not exist cannot be fought."

The blue hunters can make themselves invisible. They are born with part of this ability and learn the rest as a child.

'Gantikaya', the 'illusion', is what his clan calls this technique, which no baba knows how to use. Omu is a master of it and can immerse himself com-pletely in his surroundings' light, shadow, color, and brilliance with playful ease, to be part of the visible and not to stand out. He has learned to be swal-lowed up by what is already there: the rock, the tree, the ground, the moss, the fern. He manages never to be where the pursuer is looking, to move with the wind, sway with branches, blend in, disguise himself, flow with the current of life, yet be imperceptible and inaudible.

The spirit of camouflage masks his form. A trunk, a stone, a bush, a water-fall—everything provides him with cover. Leaves, foliage, flowers, bark, and earth stick to his skin, and they are dyed with ore pigments. Body and spirit unite, and everything merges.

Once his being has reached this state, the time has come: he and nature are one. Then, he looks at the pursuer, who is left alone, now searching for the invisible in the midst of his sphere.

Omu's sense of hearing reveals that three men, each with a leashed dog, are entering the forest. Even at this distance, he can see how clumsily and awkwardly they move through the branches. The dogs are not yet off-leash. He has to transform quickly to become invisible.

He turns inward and summons the image: "Gantikaya!"

He promptly scores the trunk of a larch tree with his hunting knife, tears off a piece of bark, scrapes out reddish-golden resin and smears the sticky tree sap on his torso and limbs. He sticks a small, hard lump into his mouth and chews on it happily.

In no time at all, he had collected plant parts, leaves, soil, pieces of bark, and grasses and attached the image of the natural environment to himself. He dipped his face with colored pigment residue from his bag.

In an instant, Omu is completely camouflaged, his form concealed, and his spirit becomes one with the forest, merging with the wilderness and his ancestors.

In front of everyone, Kela gently placed the bullet in Watka's wrinkled hand and tried to smile as innocently as possible. The old woman nodded in understanding and murmured something in her language. Then, she turned to Lilly and Walker.

"Our Kela has averted evil from you. The discovery of a bullet in Meru's chest would have surely meant that you would have incurred the wrath of my people. But now, you have proven that you're nothing like that dead intruder. For that, we thank you."

Lilly stroked the young Stone Age woman's arm, while Walker was made to lie down on a clean straw mat, where a woman powdered with lime dabbed his graze with the essence of yarrow and medicinal mushrooms. The light-colored liquid stopped the bleeding and prevented gangrene. The sister then applied a bluish paste that smelled of honey and arnica, carefully placed dry moss on top, and bandaged the whole thing with a soft, finely perforated strip of leather.

Meanwhile, two burly green-faced Neanderthals were sorting out the ammunition from Stolin's belongings and anything made of steel, plastic or glass, including a small galvanized foot trap they found in his kneepad pocket, his valuable hunting knife with a Damascus blade, his wristwatch and his marching compass, which seemed so unworldly and threatening to them that they prepared to smash it with a stone on the ground as a precaution. Walker stopped them at the last second. They stowed the objects in a kind of woven backpack, which they demonstratively placed at the Australian's feet.

"When you leave, take it with you," Watka urged them. "We don't want it. It won't burn at the stake like him. Take the murderer's gun, too.

That way, it won't bring us any harm."

Walker nodded in agreement. A boy of about ten years old was dragging a waterskin with drinking water, and a girl with flowers in her hair had a leather sack full of provisions. At that moment, Lilly thought of the horses, which were undoubtedly thirsty. It was time to set off.

The brown buffalo horn hung from Watka's shoulder on a long, smooth leather strap. Still wearing Walker's hat, Kela sidled up to the old woman, tugged on the strap, and spoke pleadingly to her until Watka took the horn off and handed it to Lilly with both hands.

"Kela wants me to give this to you. Our people call it *yu-woo*, which means *call of life*. When Omu hears the horn, he will come. We all long for him. He is our best hunter and should become our leader. It may look busy down here, but our people are small in number. They need every soul, and they especially need him. Kela pines for her husband. Bring him home as you brought home the spearhead!"

"I understand, Watka," Lilly said sadly as she stowed the horn away. "We can't promise we'll succeed, but we'll try as hard as we possibly can." They thanked each other warmly and said goodbye.

"Know that we will not betray you or this place," Walker assured Old Watka. "You can count on that! We're aware that the wilderness is suffering. Day after day and night after night, man exploits it, penetrating every nook and cranny, conquering it piece by piece and reshaping it as he sees fit. He must never come this far. May you remain hidden forever!"

The wrinkled, blue-faced woman seemed relieved. She gave Kela a brief, stern look and nodded as if to signal that some monumental agreement had been signed. The young Neanderthal woman dutifully took the Akubra and put it back on Walker's head.

"Arub-kweppu-tsi-tik," she said with a few clicking noises, looking melancholy.

"She returns it to you with thanks," Watka translated. "Because it doesn't belong in her world."

Walker adjusted his hat with satisfaction and quickly hugged the little girl. "Goodbye, good child!"

"Jarin-ko Omu," Kela asked, and everyone knew what she meant.

A burly hunter led Lilly and Walker to the entrance cave. As they stepped out through the waterfall, he held an umbrella of large magnolia leaves over them.

On the other side, the mountain lake lay as peacefully as before. They were back in the outside world and knew that the desire to return would accompany them for the remainder of their days.

The hunter stayed behind them, smudging all the footprints with a duster. When they reached the horses, they turned back to him, but he was gone. Surprisingly, he had already left the waterskin with the animals. How he had managed to pass them twice on the narrow path without them noticing would keep them wondering for a long time.

"I've also brought a little surprise," said Lilly, pulling a smartphone from the inside pocket of her vest with a wink. "Only for *absolute* emergencies. Whatever you think of Elon Musk, I will call Fred now using his ingenious Starlink."

In a stoic calm, Omu awaits the high-headed men with their little humanized wolves, which they call dogs. The dogs are just like their masters, the foolish bobos, the high-headed men; their bond with nature is severed, and their sixth sense stunted. They have lost their understanding of the ancient web of life. For too long, their existence developed outside of nature. They are awkward when they enter the wilderness because it is foreign to them.

The small human wolves will arrive first. They are light-footed, and there are three of them. He has to face them and will not flee, but he is poorly armed without an axe. So, sitting in the thicket, he carves another heavy, arm-length oak branch to defend himself. His mind wanders, flying to his people like a king buzzard over the primeval valley.

From the air, he sees Kela kneeling in front of a blue-faced corpse. She looks up at him and calls out imploringly: "Ja-ni, wu-ma, mat-ki!"

Omu hears the words clearly and distinctly. He knows the words but does not understand their meaning.

"What do you want to tell me?" he asks.

"Ja-ni, wu-ma, mat-ki!" she calls out again.

The distance is too great. Omu flies down to her, embraces her with his wings, and feels her small, robust body that belongs only to him. Now, her warm, sweet breath is very close to his ear.

"Say it one last time," he asks her.

Then, she calls out so loudly that he jumps in fright: "Ja-ni, wu-ma, mat-ki!"

He suddenly comes to his senses. He has finally understood. Kela called out the names of the three poisons to him: the poison of the frog, the poison of the mushroom and the poison of the snake. Old Watka taught them how to use these poisons, especially in times of need. His love has now reminded him of this over the great distance.

There is not much time. Omu digs into the soil, sniffs it, then tastes it on his tongue. He lifts his gaze to the treetops, weighing the rustle of needles and leaves, while the air hums with the drone of beetles and flies. What are the voices of the forest telling him?

There are no poisonous frogs here. Poisonous snakes are also undetectable. But he has picked up on the scent of mushrooms. He senses a breeze and walks toward it. Two birch trees are growing in a tiny clearing a few steps away. Small mushrooms with light green caps are growing around their white trunks. He quickly stuffs one into his pocket.

"Thank you, Kela!"

He waits by the trees, listening to the sounds of the attackers. The dogs are free now, rushing ahead of their owners in his direction. His muscular, heavy body tenses. Resin in his palm gives him a firm grip on the club. He is both the hunted and the hunter.

"Gantikaya!"

The first dog dashes toward the clearing. Smaller than the wolves he is used to, this human wolf is agile and fast. He can't see Omu, rushes past him, turns in irritation, picks up the scent again, and makes one last leap. Out of nowhere, Omu's club hits his forehead.

The snarling animal falls to the ground like a pinecone. But, like a pine-cone falling from a tree, it is still alive. That's good! Omu nimbly stuffs a small piece of greenling mushroom into the unconscious dog's mouth. The poison will take effect slowly. The animal will be sick for days. He will recover, but by that time, Omu hopes to be far, far away.

Immediately afterward, the next human wolf leaps toward the birch trees, scenting its prey close by. When it is within range, Omu strikes its hind leg. The hock tears and the leg shatters like rotten wood. The dog writhes howls in pain, and wriggles like a fish out of water. Omu grabs him nimbly by the scruff and uses the club handle to push part of the mushroom into his howling mouth. Then, he leaves him.

The last dog is now there. He followed the movements in the fight. That's why he can see Omu. He barks wildly, circles him, and dodges back and forth with agility. But it does not attack.

There is no time. The bobo men are following the barking. Soon, they will be there, too.

"Come on, little wolf! Come here!"

The furious four-legged friend keeps a safe distance. Omu hurls the club at it. The agile animal ducks and the club narrowly misses, but now it seizes its chance. With a short approach, it leaps toward Omu in a high arc. In a flash, Omu reaches for the holster with his left hand and grabs the handle of the hunting knife. At the same time, he wriggles out of the dog's trajectory.

Sharper than beaver's teeth, the flint edge drives smoothly through the flank of the passing dog. Screeching, it hits the ground and somersaults across the forest floor. The searing pain in its side will teach him never to attack Omu again.

Carrying their weapons in front of them, the three men reach the place of battle moments later. Stunned, they find the defeated dogs. They look for the perpetrator and search through the nearby bushes. Although he is standing close to them, they do not recognize Omu. Distraught and at a loss, they carry their injured little human wolves back to the familiar safety of the indoors.

Fred was glued to the panoramic window, watching in amazement as the demoralized SWAT team loaded up their whimpering search dogs and hurried off. There was no sign of Omu.

With his mood suddenly elevated to levels he hadn't experienced in many a month, he heated up a frozen lasagna and ate. Despite his joy, he missed the Neanderthal; he was, after all, his own real superhero—even if only for a night.

He reached Tom via the walkie-talkie. Together, they checked around the enclosures, took four wheelbarrows of fresh meat out of the camp, and fed the hungry wolves. Afterward, the Wolf Cub headed up to Deer Hill, where orchids were in bloom. Fred took a shower and tried unsuccessfully to reach Lilly.

Stan announced his visit at short notice. He looked a little shaken when he arrived. "Where is he?" he wanted to know urgently. "Where is Omu? It's serious!"

Fred poured him a double whiskey—he didn't need to ask whether it was needed—and described in full detail the ordeal that had happened.

"Omu outsmarted me again, but he didn't do anything to me. He's peaceful, really. Then, the FBI rolled up, and suddenly, he was gone— just, like, *poooof…* vanished into thin air. He's still out there somewhere. Unfortunately, they found his stone axe next to the crate. Then, they went into the woods with three Belgian Malinois to look for him. I couldn't do anything. They told me to stay put. I had to make coffee for them. I only put a *tiny* bit of powder in it, so it tasted awful."

Stan smelled the whiskey and shuddered; the stuff wasn't for him, but the way it calmed his nerves made the taste partially bearable.

"Didn't the Malinois get him?"

"Ha! You should've seen it. After three-quarters of an hour, the search team returned and reloaded the dogs."

"Reloaded?"

"Oh yes. They couldn't get into the back on their own. The poor guys were beaten up pretty badly. One was bleeding from the flank, another was unconscious and had a sprained leg, and the third was throwing up all sorts of things. It was quite a sight."

"Omu overpowered three Belgian Shepherds, the world's smartest dogs?"

"Even better, he left them alive, just incapacitated them. It's like I told you...he is not a monster. He could've killed them doggos if he wanted. Heck, he could've killed me and you if he wanted, too."

"I don't think they care much about his character, Fred."

"Well, at least he achieved one thing: they ran off. The entire unit left *immediately*. They didn't even say thank you. They were frustrated and not just because the coffee tasted watery."

Stan put the empty whiskey glass down on the table. "Now they know he has, how shall I put it, superhuman abilities. They'll adjust to that. They won't give up, you know. On the contrary!"

"Oh, you're half-right. But you didn't see what I saw. Omu taught them to be afraid," Fred said rather proudly. "They won't be back that quickly."

Stan ran his hands nervously through his hair. "Two came into my office and gave me a work over. They were talking about national security like there was a monster on the loose.

They asked a thousand questions. But I didn't mention Omu at all."

"Good job, Stan."

"But I had to tell them something. I told them about my visit to prison."

"You were in prison?"

"Well, kind of. I was there to learn about archaic hunting methods from one of the inmates."

"Archaic methods? You mean... lances, spears, bows, arrows, that sort of thing?"

"Exactly. The man's name is Jack Manchin. I thought he would help me somehow. And when I told the special agent about it, he was suddenly very interested in the man and asked me where exactly he was serving time and for what."

"And what is he in there for?"

"He's a notorious poacher. And I mean *notorious*. Shoots everything in sight. Ruthless and cunning."

"Nasty combination."

"When it comes to hunting, he's an old hand. That's his profession. He didn't get caught for years. But in the end, he did."

"That's normally the way. But why would the FBI be interested in him?"

Stan looked worried. "After what happened with the dogs... I think they could use someone like him in this situation."

"But he's in jail."

The ranger shook his head regrettably. "I'm afraid that when it comes to national security, they're allowed to get him out of there. They'll offer him a pardon and use him for themselves."

"As a bounty hunter? That would be bad. Do you think he'd go for it?"

There was no need to answer. The gravel outside crunched again as the silver Bronco SUV skidded to a halt in front of the building.

A cloud of dust enveloped the vehicle. Jonathan Foul and two other agents got out of the back. The driver, a lanky fellow, jumped out of the front seat, sprinted around to the passenger door, and opened it like a chauffeur.

After a few long seconds, Jack Manchin stepped out of the haze and onto the courtyard. He was wearing a dark brown marten-skin coat that almost touched the ground, black Cavallo hunting boots, and a dark baseball cap. For a while, he stood there with his arms folded, looking around like a gladiator in the circular arena of the Colosseum, taking stock of his hostile surroundings. His insensitive, bright blue eyes peered unabashedly through the wide panoramic window behind which Fred and Stan were standing. He had noticed them.

Stan didn't dare move. A queasy feeling overcame him. From now on, the poacher was no longer under the supervision of the prison guards. At large, he made an almost homicidal impression. "Speak of the devil!"

"Oh my god. Darth Vader!" said Fred. "Look at the others! They're all courting him."

Like ants around their queen, the four FBI officers swarmed around their leader. Foul pointed to the forest and spoke urgently to Manchin. The lanky driver removed his coat and helped him into a bulletproof vest. Another officer spread a map in front of him, and the fourth dragged a large hard-case suitcase from the back of the SUV.

Manchin snatched the box from his hands, heaved it onto the back of the pick-up, and turned the combination lock until the lid popped open. The routine and agility with which he opened it and handled the equipment inside made it clear that the FBI had provided him with his hunting equipment. He immediately counted and checked that every-thing was in the right place. Without wasting any time, he took out his Winchester Model 70, fitted and screwed the scope and other parts to it, and stowed plenty of ammunition in his pockets.

"I can't watch this," said Fred indignantly. "They want to hunt down Omu!"

The ring of a cell phone could be heard, so he hurried to the main office and grabbed the phone off the coffee table. Lilly was calling from Montana.

"We're on our way back!"

Fred almost started crying with relief. "Ms. Feron," he stammered, "there's a... a Neanderthal here."

"That's good news, Freddy."

"His name is Omu."

"I know."

"You *know*?"

"We know his people. We visited them. Just between us, it's legend-ary. Don't tell anyone about it! Leave Omu in peace! We'll take him back to his family."

"But there's hardly any time! He's hiding in the forest. The authori-ties are here too. I think they want to hunt him down. They're here with some professional hunter, or something"

"No, they can't do that, Fred. Don't let them! Stop them from doing it, Freddy!"

"How am I supposed to do that, boss? Help me!"

"Come up with something! Make some noise! Warn him! Be proactive!"

"Okay, I'll try. I'll try. You know, he's my friend."

"That's good, Fred. I'm counting on you. You're doing good!"

"I'll do what I can."

"Proud of you!"

Lilly ended the call. Fred ran off, got something from his room, and returned to the kitchen. Stan remained frozen at the window. A gray Ford Raptor growled to a halt outside, and two armed figures spilled out, moving with predatory intent. One of them looked like a Native American. He was carrying a modern longbow and hunting arrows. The other wore a black headband and a Rambo T-shirt, holding his over-sized Bowie knife.

"Nice guys," said Fred.

The men knew the poacher personally. They greeted him reverently and were immediately given tactical instructions.

"There are three of them," Stan said. "Heavily armed. Omu doesn't stand a chance. I think one of them is a Shadow Wolf, a tracker."

Stan recognized the badge on the Indian-looking man's camouflage suit, a beige coat of arms with the words Homeland Security Investigations Special Agent and an eagle spreading its wings above it. He was a descendant of one of the six other Indian tribes that made up the famous Shadow Wolves special unit. Jack Manchin now had an actual specialist with him.

"If the other two don't get him, the Shadow Wolf will," said Stan. "Dead certain!"

"They're not allowed to do that!" Fred shouted angrily. "My boss has forbidden it!" A small backpack hung on his shoulder. "I'm going to make a bit of a racket. Our wolves won't like it, but maybe I can warn Omu," he said, holding out his open hand to Stan. "Lighter, please!"

Stan pulled his lighter out of his breast pocket and handed it to Fred. "What on earth are you up to? Don't do anything stupid!"

"I'm going to celebrate a little New Year's Eve."

After finishing the final sip of his whiskey, Fred ran along the corridor into a side part of the building, unlocking the door to a small backyard. Outside was the camper van that served as the Wolf Cub's accommodation. Behind it was a ladder attached to the front of the house. It led up to the roof. The trainee, who did not have a good head for heights, took a deep breath and climbed up. Before Stan could catch up with him, he was already at the top.

"What the hell are you doing?" he shouted from below.

The roof was steeper than expected, and the surface was not entirely grippy. On all fours, Fred slowly crawled up one side to the ridge. He was forced to turn one hundred eighty degrees and crawl to the opposite side of the roof at the highest point. His heart was pounding. All he could see was the roof and the sky.

He inched forward, muscles taut. At the roof's edge, he lowered himself into a seat, heart hammering. Below stretched the forest and the park's enclosures, the entrance, and part of the courtyard. One side of the square pressed against a wolf enclosure; the rest dissolved into shadowy trees. Twenty feet beneath him, the men's voices carried, sharp and oblivious to his presence.

Now, he thought, *I'm going to turn up the heat.*

The backpack was full of New Year's Eve firecrackers. It had been sitting untouched in the corner of his room for years. In his first year of apprenticeship, he bought the firecrackers for a New Year's Eve party, but Lilly had forbidden him to light them in the wolf park. He now understood why and was ashamed to have been so naive. Above all that, though, he felt grateful to have held onto them.

He had always been most impressed by cannon crackers. They were triaxial, thick, tightly wrapped, glued with hemp twine, and made a wonderfully loud, dull bang. MADE IN CHINA, it said. He thought being used in Utah would have fitted, too, as he counted them. There were six, alongside dozens of match firecrackers and countless small Chinese firecrackers. *This should be enough.*

He removed one cannon cracker and made a hollow inside the other firecrackers. Then, he carefully pulled the small plastic cap off the thick, short fuse of the cannon cracker and placed it in the center of the hollow. Now, all he had to do was light the string of the cube, close the zipper, and throw everything down. He didn't have to throw it far, as the eaves of the roof were only about three feet away. The agents were probably right underneath.

He went through the three simple steps again:

Light the string—close the rucksack—throw the backpack

After the explosion, he would simply stay on the roof and wait to see what happened. Then he got to work.

Lighting them was easy. Fred struck the fuse and shoved Stan's lighter into his backpack—then the zipper jammed. The bag caught on him, scraped the roof, and a small cloud of smoke hissed up.

The charge was already burning. He had to move—now!

He hastily grabbed the bag and tried to throw it again, but it stuck to him like a burr. Now, he realized in horror that his shirt sleeve was stuck in the zipper. Oh, no!

Panicking, he tried to kick it off with his feet. His upper body swung to the side. He searched desperately for support but found none. He rolled around, tumbled helplessly, slipped off the edge of the roof, and hurtled down screaming.

Part of the New Year's Eve surprise exploded next to him in free fall. At least the sturdy backpack had withstood the explosion instead of bursting. Fred had miscalculated that, too.

Its impact in the bushes of the front garden was louder than the muffled bang of the firecrackers. He briefly lost consciousness.

The sound of laughter brought him out of his blackout. Firecrackers were still exploding as he crawled around, looking for his horn-rimmed glasses. As soon as he struggled to get up, two of the FBI agents dragged him out into the yard by his collar. One of them zip-tied his wrists and ankles and pinned him down. Fred sat on the ground, a filthy and embarrassed mess with hair full of leaves.

"What's this supposed to be? A cute little terrorist attack?" the agent teased scornfully.

"Sit here and don't move, understand? We've been suspicious of you all along. You just messed your life up, buddy."

Stan came out of the house and ran across the courtyard to his friend. "You okay, Buddy?"

"I'll survive."

Jonathan Foul recognized Stan immediately. He had only questioned him that morning. "Do we have an accomplice here?" he asked smugly.

Outraged, Stan pulled out his clothes brush, pointed it at the FBI officer and said belligerently: "I'll have you know that this is an unauthorized hunt and therefore illegal."

"Illegal and reckless," Fred encouraged him, groaning in pain. "They don't even know what they're hunting!"

"Then, you tell me, smart guy!" Foul challenged him harshly. "Tell me, what's out there?"

"No one you need to be afraid of. Unless you make him angry. Which, by the way, you're going the right way about."

"He's right, Mr. Foul." Stan tried to sound balanced. "Just leave him alone! We'll find a way to resolve the matter peacefully with common sense instead of aggression."

"What are you suggesting?" asked Foul tartly. "An invitation to a self-discovery course? Psychological dialog? Didn't you see what that monster did to our dogs?"

"He let them live," Fred said calmly. "He was just defending himself. No need to send a bounty hunter after him… 'specially one who doesn't care what he hunts as long as he gets enough for it."

"That's right!" shouted Jack Manchin. "Now shut your mouth, boy! I'm warning you, don't mess with me!"

"We'll continue as planned," Jonathan Foul ordered his team. "Just as the FBI directorate in Washington has approved."

Stan knew that the fact that the case had been discussed at FBI headquarters showed its level of priority. Stan nevertheless persisted. He had gotten to know Omu. Lynching him was simply unthinkable.

"Let's at least try it," he pleaded again.

Now, the poacher was bursting at the seams, hungry for a kill. With the Winchester in the crook of his arm, he stomped toward the ranger belligerently and stood before him. His breath smelled intensely of chewing tobacco.

"Nothing there!" he drooled. "Too late for the soft touch. You instigated this whole thing yourself and came to my prison cell. The FBI and I have a deal now, and I'm gonna do my part… whether there's a T-rex, a lunatic, a vampire, or whatever out there. I don't care what it is; I'll find it and hunt it down. And a puppet like you can't damn well stop me."

Increasingly angry and standing with his finger on the trigger, he seemed to be threatening everyone present. He was seething with rage, showing his dark, diabolical side. With his freedom at stake, he would not be stopped at any price.

His followers stood submissively beside him, none daring to say anything. The bounty hunter spat contemptuously on the ground and wiped his mouth with his sleeve.

"Terry and Akecheta, let's go get him!"

Oblivious to the events unfolding around him, Tom, the Wolf Cub, strolled down the narrow pass from Deer Hill through Goshawk forest to the polar wolf enclosure. He knows every bush and stone in this area like the back of his hand. On countless walks, his Uncle Leo had shown him the paths and forest aisles that the settlers had created decades before the wolf park was built.

In the nineteenth century, the upper soil layer of the narrow pass had been compacted by the timber industry's wagon wheels and the constant wear and tear from the hooves of draught and pack animals. It had also been washed out during heavy rainfall. Tom thought the narrow path looked like the rain gutter of the dwellings of giant, mystical forest dwellers who might still be at home here.

He was not afraid of giants, dwarves, or wild animals. On the contrary, he saw himself as closer to them than to most humans. For the same reasons, he felt safe and unassailable in the wilderness, not least because his chosen kin was a pack of snarling timber wolves.

Shortly after arriving in the Salt Lake Valley, pioneers set up the first sawmills in the nearby canyons. Utah businessmen profited from this, and logging progressed dramatically. By 1880, however, logging had reached a sad peak; the destruction of the forest had reached a critical point.

Initially, the U.S. government did little to effectively regulate grazing on forest lands until influential private organizations provided the necessary support. The result was the Forest Reserve Act of 1891 and the Organic Act of 1897, which authorized the U.S. President to establish forest reserves to protect timber and watersheds. Finally, forests and wetlands could be sustainably protected.

The forest around Feron Wolf Park also gradually recovered. Only the clearing on Deer Hill still bore witness to the clear-cutting of the nineteenth century. Lilly had loved the colorful meadow since her childhood. She ensured that it was kept clear and mowed regularly, as it served the veterinary clinic as a landing pad for rescue helicopters in emergencies.

After her father's death, she continued walking with the Wolf Cub as often as possible. Tom didn't talk much, but he was a very good listener. Lilly often thought that her wondrous blond cousin was perhaps much more intelligent than he seemed. But he didn't follow the usual social cues, so she spoke about the things that fascinated her: Konrad Lorenz and behavioral research; Rachel Carson, the mother of ecology; astrobiology, which deals with man's origin in the universe; and, more than anything, the wolves that shaped her and Tom's daily life in equal measure.

As a doctor, she also knew about the proven healing effects of the forest. The topic had nothing to do with magic or romance. Instead, Lilly could explain the positive effects on health from a scientific perspective.

"Spending time in the forest is a complete healing package," she told Tom. "A real elixir of life, not to mention a boost for our immune system. We've been assuming this for a long time. But now, with science, we understand *why* that is the case." She bent down and took a piece of green-brown soil in her hand. "Can you smell that, Tom? Do you smell the earth and the moss?"

Tom stood by her and inhaled the delicate scents of the forest.

"You know, breathing this in is like taking medicine. Only, the factories that make this medicine live underground. They are tiny bacteria called streptomyces. They produce natural antibiotics on the forest floor.

Then, they release molecules of these healing substances into the air. You can't see them, but they fly around everywhere. When you smell forest soil, it's these molecules. We call their scent geosmin. So, you're breathing in a natural antibiotic!"

"Geosmin smells good," said Tom, spreading his arms and filling his lungs.

"I think so, too. As you know, some diseases, such as cancer or viral diseases, are complicated to cure. Our body defends itself against them with its killer cells in the blood. If we are sick, we need many of these defense cells. And this is exactly where the forest air helps us. It contains phytoncides—basically, chemical substances that trees and other plants use to protect themselves. These phytoncides stimulate humans and animals to produce more killer cells."

"I haven't counted, but I've probably got a lot of them in my blood. I'm always in the forest."

"That's right, my dear. You are certainly healthier and more energetic than your brother in the big city."

"I have a brother in the big city?"

"Not really," Lilly replied and laughed. "For comparison's sake!"

That's how they talked on their walks together. Today, however, Tom was walking alone. He didn't need much company because, like the forest and everything in it, he could cope independently.

He rescued a shimmering blue beetle from a puddle, left the narrow pass, and reached the fence around the polar wolves. He couldn't explain why they were excitedly sprinting through the spacious area today. The eight white four-legged creatures were fascinating, but the unapproachable pack left him feeling like he could not access them physically or emotionally.

Three hundred feet ahead began the enclosure of his familiar timber wolves, who were already waiting for him, whimpering and whistling. As they were reared by hand, they were not wary of contact. Tom often pressed his body against the wire mesh so that they could be very close to him. The biggest males towered far above him when they stood up against the fence.

He usually had a few treats, which also proved helpful in many situations. Today, he stuffed worming tablets into the chicken livers Fred had given him and put his medication through the wire mesh into each animal's mouth. *Eat, my friends!*

He was just as fearless with the timber wolves as he was with Omu when he unexpectedly appeared at the fence beside him. The autistic man noted the Neanderthal's strange shape, but it didn't worry him; he intuitively knew that this being was not frightening. The pack on the other side of the fence also behaved as if the early man were a loyal friend, a soulmate—nothing but another Wolf Cub.

Like a little boy wanting to feed his pet, Tom reached into his pocket with his right hand, pulled out a leftover chicken liver and held it in front of Omu's broad, fleshy nose. Grunting in a friendly manner, Omu happily ate from his hand. *Eat, my friend!*

A pack of half-tame timber wolves, an autistic man with savant syndrome, and a genuine Neanderthal—three beings, three species, yet moving in silent understanding, as if some invisible thread bound them together. They stayed together for a few more seconds, then Omu stroked the Wolf Cub's light hair tenderly, moved away and disappeared silently into the undergrowth.

47

The encounter with the young bobo touched Omu's heart. He couldn't get him out of his head. A yellow fuzz covered his delicate head. He appeared as innocent as he was vulnerable, radiating an unclouded familiarity and being a friend to the captive wolves. Truth shone in his eyes, and an immaculate heartbeat was in his chest.

As if they had been connected for a long time, the young bobo tolerated Omu's closeness without fear, even feeding him and showing him affection, as if familiar with the customs of the primeval valley. Omu recognized the kindness and purity of this soul. He stroked his golden-colored stubble thoughtfully before dipping back into the forest.

Now, Omu hears a scream, a muffled bang, and a thud and suspects it's the redhead. Fred is in danger! He has to get back to bobo's den.

On the way there, his keen sense of hearing detects three pursuers combing through the forest. He bypasses them undetected and reaches the courtyard in front of the dwelling. There, the redhead sits tied up on the ground. His gaunt friend is with him. Four indifferent figures with yellow markings on their clothes stand slightly to one side. They are talking to each other and seem distracted. Omu takes advantage of this, sneaks up on Fred from the opposite side, bites through his bonds and whispers, "Frett galu."

He had just freed him when a thunder of angry wolf barking echoed from the forest. In a flash, Omu sees a vision in which the young, innocent bobo is harmed. He runs back to the trapped wolves as fast as possible, but he is too late! The bobo lies helpless on the ground while one of the pursuers, wearing a black headband, stabs the bobo with a large knife.

They want Omu, and an innocent man has been hit because of it.

Shouting angrily, the primeval hunter bends down to grab a fist-sized rock. Noticing this, the man with the knife, a stone's throw away, lets go of his victim in irritation, jumps up and tries to run away. He doesn't get far. At full speed, Omu hits him in the neck. Neck vertebrae splinter and his fragile head moves to the side. The victim falls, but he is not dead. Groaning, he struggles to his feet and drags himself forward on all fours.

The trapped wolves witness everything. They try to dig themselves free, try to jump as high as possible. Separated from his pack, the young bobo lies motionless as his blood soaks into the earth. But he is still breathing. Omu gently presses the green shepherd's purse into the wounds.

"Bana-t-ki-maku," he mumbles, "don't die!"

Omu's fury explodes. With a roar, he releases the wolves. They leap instantly, tearing the crawling man apart; his screams shriek like a piglet's before cutting off abruptly.

Omu kneels and lifts the injured young bobo. The wolves circle, howling, then fall into submission, trailing him as he carries him back to the house.

48

Special Agent Jonathan Foul and his colleagues sat in the silver Bronco, eating soggy sandwiches. The balmy summer air blew through the open vehicle doors, and a great spotted woodpecker knocked on a tree somewhere. This made work fun, Foul thought, and he was already very proud of himself.

"Clever of me to let that poacher do the dirty work, eh boys?" he threw haughtily into the circle, earning ardent approval.

The employees had a fair amount of respect for Foul, their SWAT team leader; however, that was based on an event long ago. In the 1990s, when the FBI arrested the famous Unabomber, Theodore Kaczynski, in his cabin in rural Montana, Jonathan Foul had just joined the Salt Lake City Division as a very young agent. This very division carried out the same operation.

As a newbie, he was completely uninvolved in the terrorist's arrest. Nevertheless, he was subsequently mentioned by name here and there in the press. He knew how to use this skillfully. Over time, he meticulously collected all the articles in which his name appeared. Gradually, he twisted the facts in his favor, telling the story in a way that suited him perfectly. He did this until he finally believed in his own tales of heroism.

Some of his superiors noticed this supposed achievement. They appointed him a special agent and the Special Activities Division of the US Secret Service registered him as a Specialized Skills Officer. This meant he was authorized by the highest authority to carry out certain special operations in full secrecy. With this backing, he acted in this position outside the legal system. His remit even included powers to deceive and evade law enforcement agencies.

Of course, he was forbidden to brag about this publicly, and he certainly didn't cover himself in glory in his regular professional career. So, all he could do was cultivate his image, which made him happy.

He was instructed to track down and neutralize the unknown, highly dangerous 'subject' from the very top. The day before, Foul had received a call from the J. Edgar Hoover Building in Washington, D.C. The FBI director himself was on the phone. He immediately classified the case as top-secret, offering Foul a description of the target as a "biological time bomb." The agent had not received much more information, but it showed the explosive nature of the matter.

Fortunately, the job was simply a license to kill. That suited him just fine. Foul was only a month off retirement, and he was quietly hoping for a final assignment that had the potential to polish his reputation in what little time remained. He craved an infamous story he could tell as a pensioner at the pool bar, sipping on a vodka martini between each line. This special operation was his last opportunity to do so. It was supposed to go smoothly and gloriously.

Since the FBI is responsible for the preliminary investigation of possible threats regardless of concrete suspicion, Foul's task force did not require further powers. He had the necessary leeway. Only the work in the forest posed a moderate problem, as neither he nor his colleagues were experienced hunters.

Coincidentally, however, this lanky ranger, Stan Hardy, was carelessly chatting during the interrogation about his prison meeting with a knowledgeable poacher named Jack Manchin. Foul recognized the opportunity and enlisted the convict immediately. It went like clockwork. Now, all he had to do was seal the deal.

"Make it look like a hunting accident," he instructed the poacher. "Gladly," Manchin had replied. He didn't even ask for money; he just wanted his freedom back. Foul was certain that, together with his assistants, the man would deliver. After that, he could pick up where he left off as a poacher, and make all the money he desired.

The snack break suddenly ended.

"Be quiet!" said one of the agents, speaking from the corner of a full mouth. "I think they've got him."

Everyone stopped chewing and listened. Foul got out of the car.

"Sounds like it!" he confirmed, listening to the deadly screams from the forest.

He took it as a promising sign that his plan was working and that the hitman and his helpers were executing the 'biological time bomb' at that very moment. This meant he didn't have to stumble around in the wilderness. He had always been suspicious of it and preferred the city. In any case, he now felt too big and old for such adventurous activities.

He looked down at his stomach. Mayonnaise had dripped onto his T-shirt. He picked it up with his finger, licked it off contentedly, rubbed the grease stain, huffed, and lit a cigarette. *It's going well*, he thought. Soon, Manchin's men would bring in the dead man. All his SWAT team had to do was take the body's blood and fingerprints, photograph it, and wrap it in sterile bags before transporting it. There was a supply of body bags in the car. Then, he would call the FBI director and report success.

A few minutes passed, and silence returned. They would show up at any moment. Foul looked around. There was no sign of Stan and the cheeky red-haired guy. They had probably cut the zip ties and disappeared into the house. He didn't care. Two young dogs were wrestling at the edge of the large, dusty courtyard. *Cute*, he thought, *such beautiful, long legs!* A larger dog stood about sixty-five feet away and looked at him calmly.

Something feels kinda off.

A second, equally tall dog appeared not far from him. Then, a third appeared opposite, also staring at him silently.

Foul felt uneasy, and a cold chill ran down his spine. *What the hell!* Beads of sweat trickled down on his temples and forehead. The hairs on the back of his neck stood up as if electrified. They bristled like a mane of a wolf.

Foul wanted to swallow, but his dry throat wouldn't allow it; he tried to shout but couldn't make a sound. Decisively, he tore himself free, stumbled clumsily to the SUV, rushed inside and banged his head on the door frame. Only when he was inside did a hoarse "Wolves everywhere!" escape his lips.

His employees, equally horrified, dropped everything to slam the vehicle doors shut. Soggy white bread landed on their laps, and hot coffee from the thermos burned their thighs. "God curse it!" they shouted. "Close the doors, damn it! Hurry up! Close 'em!"

Panicking, they rolled up the windows and locked the doors. Meanwhile, the timber wolves—a dozen at least—were swarming the car. There were too many for the men to shoot them. They were trapped.

A handsome male with black fur and piercing eyes leapt elegantly onto the hood. He stared at them, bared his teeth, and scratched at the windshield. The agents clutched the backrests in fear. A mighty, light gray female wolf reared up at the side window. She banged her front legs against one of the windows, causing the car to shake, and smashed the teeth of her fearsome jaws into the side-view mirror. Up close, the size of the animal was devastating.

Minutes passed. The afternoon sun was blazing, and it quickly became stuffy in the closed vehicle's cabin. The terrorized occupants could scarcely breathe; the pungent smell of urine gave away their fear.

Logical thinking was hardly possible in this state. Only gradually did they manage to understand that they were probably safe.

"Calm down, guys!" said Foul, as if snapped out of a daze. "They can't come in here, understand? No chance of getting in, got it?"

"Where the *hell* did they come from?" asked another. He knelt on the back seat to get a better view through the rear window.

"They must have escaped from the enclosures. They're probably half-tame. Can you see it? They're not shy at all."

"Turn on the AC! I can't breathe."

"What do we do now?" asked the sinewy man behind the wheel, whose name was Brad Guinness.

"Flatten 'em, Brad!" his colleague urged.

"No, that wouldn't be right," said another. "Maybe they *are* tame. They live with these people, after all."

"Why don't you go out and see, you oaf! Why don't you feed 'em? Throw a ball, maybe the cute things'll play fetch with ya! I'll give you a hundred bucks if you do."

Foul thought about it. Finally, he ordered: "Get going, Guinness! These are dangerous beasts. If we flatten some of them, all the better. The others will get away. Let's show them who's boss!"

Guinness obediently started the engine, shifted into drive, and was about to pull away when the heavy SUV lifted sideways with a jolt. An incredibly bulky skull with a gruff face appeared at the side door. The agents were utterly aghast. The bizarre creature had shoved a thick, ten-foot-long branch between the front and rear axles and was levering the vehicle upward like a toy.

Clutching the steering wheel, Guinness stepped on the gas. The engine revved, and the tires spun. Omu pushed the car a little higher, jumped back at the last moment, and pulled the branch with him. The SUV skidded forward on two wheels for a short distance. Guinness tried to counter-steer but turned the wheel in the wrong direction, causing the SUV to tilt even more, pass the tipping point and crash onto its side. The occupants tumbled down, falling on each other and wedging each other in place.

"*Gorighuuuai!*" Omu made a loud, shuddering cry of victory.

Then, he ran to the patch of grass at the edge of the courtyard where he had put down Tom. He carefully carried him toward the entrance to the house. A few wolves gathered around them, nudging Omu with their cool noses.

Fred and Stan had been watching from the kitchen. Fred went to the front door to meet the two of them. He didn't fear the timber wolves; he was familiar with them. Now, he recognized the bloodied man in Omu's arms.

"Oh Lord, Tom, what have they done to you?"

The deathly pale Wolf Cub moaned in pain.

Stan continued to observe proceedings from the window. He saw a dark figure on the opposite, lightless edge of the courtyard, about one hundred and sixty-five feet away. It was Jack Manchin! In his long, dark brown coat, he flew up to the second vehicle, the Ford Raptor, like a shadow and disappeared into it without the wolves noticing him. Shortly afterward, one of the pick-up's windows rolled halfway down, and a long gun barrel emerged. Manchin was aiming at the Neanderthal.

Stan was alarmed. Something had to happen. He couldn't go into the yard because of the wolves. He banged desperately on the window-pane, but no one responded. Was there any other way?

"Come on, Stan, you can do this!"

In a flash, the old camper van came to his mind. He stormed into the side of the building and ran through the door into the backyard. There it was. The driver's door was unlocked. He climbed in. The key was in the ignition. A cloud of black smoke enveloped him as he started the car. He fastened his seatbelt and reversed out of the parking spot.

From a distance, Jack Manchin fired twice in quick succession at his victim, catching him from behind. The first bullet hit Omu's shoulder, and the second shredded his right ear and missed Fred by a hair's breadth. The Neanderthal made a snarling sound and let Tom slide into Fred's arms. *Take him, redhead!* Fred caught him, turned around and dragged him to the front door.

Hit hard, Omu buckled to the ground. Blood seeped from his bullet wounds. Kneeling in the dust, he needed a moment to regain his strength. But the poacher was relentless. Without further ado, Manchin decided to run him over. The result, he thought, would ultimately be the same: if it wasn't a hunting accident, it was a car accident.

The engine roared, and gravel went flying. The killer drove in a wide arc toward the man he had shot. Omu heard the approaching car and wanted to jump up, but his strength had left him. He closed his eyes and lowered his head. *It's the end for me, my people, and Kela!*

In an attempt to stop the attacker, the old timber wolf, Romulus, leapt at full speed in front of the pick-up's radiator grille. The animal sacrificed itself, but the truck stayed the course. Manchin concentrated on his goal, floored it, and gained pace. He had almost reached his target when he saw something speeding toward him out of the corner of his eye. He could no longer react. A few feet from Omu, the Ford Econoline broke through the hydrangeas and T-boned the Raptor with full force. The impact of the four-ton camper van was so violent that the Raptor rolled over several times before coming to rest in the middle of the courtyard and bursting into flames.

The camper came to a halt immediately. In the burning Raptor in front of Stan's eyes, the ammunition stowed inside exploded so fiercely that the windows shattered. Jack Manchin could no longer be saved.

Stan yanked off his seatbelt, snatched a small fire extinguisher from the cabin, and leapt out just as flames licked the edges—unharmed, but his heart was hammering. Apart from two smashed headlights and a slightly dented bumper, the solid vintage camper van was unscathed. Omu and the wolves were gone, leaving only the dead timber wolf in the dust.

Foul and his team painstakingly climbed out of the upper windows of the overturned SUV. The three employees dragged themselves, sweaty and panting, into the shade. Exhausted, Foul limped to the burning Raptor. There, Stan tried in vain to extinguish the fire. With his bow in hand, the Shadow Wolf approached. He stared silently into the flames. His hip quiver contained a handful of hunting arrows with shiny stainless steel tips.

"What rotten luck!" Stan said as emotionlessly as possible and loud enough for the two of them to hear. "I didn't even see him coming."

The Indian remained silent, only giving the ranger a dirty look. Foul faced the facts with his usual icy calculation. His hitman had failed, the target had slipped away, and nothing was going according to plan. However, he had no intention of throwing in the towel. His last chance would be lost and his reputation ruined once and for all. If he failed, he knew he wouldn't enjoy a single day of the early retirement that awaited him.

"He went back into the forest," said the Indian abruptly, pointing to a track in the gravel. "Mr. Manchin got him. He's bleeding from two wounds."

Foul's mood suddenly brightened. The 'biological time bomb' was shot, leaving a great trail of blood in its wake. *Perfect! It should be child's play for the Shadow Wolf to track him.* The cards were reshuffled.

"Hey, *you*, come here!" he called gruffly to the Indian, knocking the dust off his pants and smiling a little. "What's your name?"

"Akecheta."

"Akecheta is a great name! Are you Sioux?"

"Yes. Akecheta means warrior."

"Excellent! We need warriors like you now. We have to find this savage and hunt him down. Do you understand? And you're going to help us. You and your buddy. What was his name?"

"Terry. His name is Terry. But he can't come with us."

"Why not?" Foul was annoyed.

"He's dead."

Foul flinched briefly and quickly came to his senses. "I see. The screams in the forest… that was him."

"Yes, that was my friend."

"You see, Akecheta, this bastard monster has your friend on its conscience. It killed him. It killed Terry. We have to find it and take it out! Terry deserves justice!"

Akecheta looked over to the forest. "Let's leave him to bleed until tomorrow. Then I'll go and find him."

49

The four horses were so happy to see the returning riders. The light brown Morgan mare neighed excitedly and laid her head trustingly on Lilly's shoulder. They all seemed in good health, had no sunken eyes, and were thirsty but not dehydrated. They had eaten all the bushes and grasses they could reach, giving them a little moisture.

After a long drink, there was no time to waste. The sun was already high in the midday sky. Walker quickly saddled the horses, and Lilly tied the bags and lined up the animals.

The way back turned out to be easier than the way there, not least because much of the uncertainty had faded. The direction was now relatively clear. Starting from Larch Hill, they used the marching compass to find their way. Occasionally, they had to turn back and look for alternative terrain that was passable for the horses, but all in all, they were lucky—and they didn't meet a soul.

That night, they camped on a hillside overlooking a magnificent silhouette of black mountains, above which the Milky Way sparkled like a dream. They snuggled up together and marveled at the cosmic play of light, the slowly rotating starry sky, shooting stars of different colours and passing satellites.

"Warrumbungle," said Walker dreamily.

"Warrumbungle?"

"In my grandmother's language, that means *crooked mountains.* Warrumbungle National Park became Australia's first dark sky park in 2016. But my grandfather took me there much earlier. I've never forgotten it: ninety thousand square miles of nature, one hundred and twenty bird species, gray kangaroos, and complete darkness at night. Just like here in the mountains."

"It's never dark with you," Lilly whispered, cuddling up to him, in love.

There was no other way, no better way. They let themselves go, kissed and made love, and the small tent became a sea of emotions.

The following morning, Walker dumped Stolin's belongings in a deep crevice. The rattling sound of the falling rifle could still be heard for a long time. Lilly and Walker cheered like children when some of the ammunition exploded on the way down as if in a wild shootout. They considered it a well-deserved fireworks display.

"Firecrackers bring good luck!" shouted Lilly into the crevice. "Get out of here, evil spirits!"

"Landslides and rockfalls will ensure that none of this will ever see the light of day again," Walker guaranteed.

They made rapid progress and found their position on the map again. At a suitable watering hole close to Painted Rocks Lake, they unsaddled the horses, removed bags, halters, tethers and harnesses and hid all the riding equipment deep in the bush. Then, they set their four-legged friends free. They would find more than enough drinking water and food in this area.

After crossing one last hill, the lake was picturesquely surrounded by colorful rocks and wooded mountains. Lilly had silently hoped for it, but now she was jubilant: at the jetty, she saw a blue and white Cessna lying on the water.

"I told you, he's the best uncle in the world!" she exclaimed, hugging Walker and running down to the seaplane.

Miller had set up a tent, a folding chair, and a gas barbecue on the bank. He was about to pull in a wriggling trout when Lilly threw her arms around his neck.

"Uncle, you're already here," she exclaimed exuberantly. "That's so great!"

"You know, my darling," Miller replied, "after two days in the city, I wondered if it wouldn't be better to fly back, catch some trout, enjoy life at the lake and wait like a faithful dog for my little Lilly."

The three of them quickly stowed the expedition luggage and Miller's camping gear in the cargo area of the seaplane. The Cessna lifted off sluggishly from the sky-blue surface of Painted Rocks Lake.

During the ascent, Lilly told him about the fabulous starry sky over the Bermuda Mountains, the devastating snowstorm, and their failure to find Beringian wolves. She explained that they were in a hurry to return to the wolf park because of a "tiny little problem." The old pilot saw through her. He knew she was understating things.

"Lilly, my child. I've known you since you could walk, and I know there's something you don't want to tell me." They looked at each other sheepishly.

"And you don't have to, my darling. But, please, promise you'll tell me if things get too hot to handle. Helping you young people breathes new life into an old fool like me."

"You're right, Uncle," she replied, gently massaging his shoulders. "I'm sorry. There are some pretty dramatic things happening in the wolf park. We have to get back there as quickly as possible."

"I see! Do you still have your landing site on Deer Hill?"

"Yes, why?"

"Well, if you're in such a hurry and it's so dramatic... there's a cute Hummingbird on Great Salt Lake, a retired rescue helicopter. An old friend of mine recently snapped it up. I could put in a word for you... But you'll have to fly it yourself!"

"That would be great, Uncle!" exclaimed Lilly enthusiastically, giving Walker a questioning look.

The Australian didn't have to think twice: "I've got my license with me if that's what you mean."

50

The lime-scented body wash smelled wonderfully fresh. Fred felt renewed—reborn, even—carrying the pride of having saved a life yesterday under brutal conditions. After he fell from the roof, the yard turned into a battlefield: a pack of wolves had gone wild; two assassination attempts took place; Stan ingeniously crashed the camper van, and then there was the explosion.

He had retrieved the Wolf Cub from this chaos, dragged him into the headquarters, and laid him on the sofa. Thanks to Omu, the wounds had hardly bled at all. Fred had lifted Tom's upper body and pushed a large pillow underneath it, disinfected the stab wounds in his arm and stomach, applied gauze compresses, and made pressure bandages, just as he had learned from Lilly. He found an auto-injector in the clinic fridge, which he used to inject him with ten milligrams of morphine sulfate. The pain soon settled.

Tom's breathing calmed down too, and his condition seemed to stabilize. The attacker had missed vital organs. *Only a Wolf Cub could be so lucky*, Fred concluded. Not knowing what else to do, Fred gave him a little orange juice and covered him well. Then, they slept until it was light.

After his shower, he dialed Lilly's number. Amazingly, she answered the call straight away. He could barely hear her because, at the same time, he heard the helicopter noise through both his cell phone and kitchen window.

"Is that you above us?" he asked his boss.

"Yes! We're back. Is that a charred pickup truck lying upside down in the courtyard? What on earth happened?"

"All hell broke loose here."

"Fred, we're landing in two minutes. On Deer Hill. Where's the Neanderthal?"

Her question was answered by Stan Hardy, who had just stormed into the office and shouted: "Omu dragged himself into the forest. He's wounded. Foul sent the Indian after him."

Lilly understood. They had to get ahead of the hunter.

"Okay, Fred, please stay where you are. Now, it's our turn. We've got a plan."

She ended the call. The rescue helicopter was already hovering over the hill. Walker expertly lowered it and landed it gently on the hilltop.

"We'll do it like we agreed, okay?" she called out to him.

"Don't worry, I'll stay behind you."

Lilly jumped out of the cabin onto the orchid-covered meadow. Walker switched off the gearbox, and the rotor blades slowly came to a halt.

When it had become so quiet that the song of a pine siskin could be heard, she took a deep breath and blew as hard as she could into Watka's *yu-woo*. The buffalo horn didn't sound as full and majestic as it had in the primeval valley, but Lilly was hopeful that it served its purpose nonetheless. If the Neanderthal was within a few hundred feet, there was a real chance of attracting him with it, at least if Kela and the elder were to be believed.

51

Omu dug up a wild onion and took yarrow and shepherd's purse from his pouch. He had carefully chewed the medicinal plants, mixed the saliva pulp with a handful of loess and pressed the mixture onto his throbbing wounds. Then, he hid in the undergrowth.

In the morning, his senses tell him he is being followed by a lone bobo, a hunter with a keen instinct who does not trample around clumsily but stalks the blood trail like a lynx. It is difficult to fool the lynx. He can't shake him off in this state.

Caution is the order of the day!

His ear stings, and he won't be able to remove the agonizing bullet in his shoulder on his own. All hope is fading, and he no longer has the will to fight. He drags himself forward with difficulty. The sky has darkened, and he can do nothing about it. Once again, his goal seems unattainable, and his will is almost broken.

He ducks as a huge, terrifyingly loud insect—a hornet bigger than the biggest grizzly—appears high in the air. Omu hides in the hollow trunk of an old oak tree as quickly as his weakening legs will drag him there. Blood and sweat run down his tough, sunburnt skin. The enormous hornet hums into the forest, whirling leaves and twigs. Its noise is unbearable. Finally, little by little, it falls silent.

In the shelter of the oak tree, his eyes close briefly. Completely exhausted, he feels Kela, the most wonderful of all women, snuggling up to him gently and blowing softly on his aching ear.

"Do you hear it?" she asks him. "Do you hear it, my darling?"

Slowly, he comes to and listens. Through the clear breath of the silent grove, an infinitely familiar sound reaches his tattered ear—a sound that connects him to his people like an inseparable umbilical cord. Hesitantly, he peers out through the gap in the tree trunk. Above the black silhouette of the treetops, the sky clears as if this proud, sustaining sound were blowing away all the black veils. Darkness gives way to light, and suddenly, he realizes what he is hearing:

"Yu-woo," he whispers with joy. "The sound of the buffalo horn!"

The horn of his people sounds when a child is born in the primeval valley, when a brother's life ends, or when a gatherer has lost her way in the mountains. Everyone follows its call, which unites his people like the cliffs of the primeval valley and the sacred spear around which they gather.

The comforting sound comes from the direction of the big hornet. Omu didn't mess around. Without suspecting what awaits him, he follows it. His legs carry him instinctively. He has nothing to lose, has no fear, and does not look back.

A large wolf with bright hawk eyes trots ahead as if showing him the way through the thicket to his destination.

52

"Come on, come here, my friend!" Lilly implored the lost hunter and blew her horn again, hoping Omu would hear her.

Her experiences in the primeval valley stayed with her forever. Kela's enchanting personality and the extraordinary otherness of her obscure brothers and sisters were forever etched in her heart.

As a biologist, she constantly wondered how to classify these creatures. Of course, Neanderthals did not fit into the animal world. Without question, they were human, but they were fundamentally different from all humans living today—far more so than any other ethnic group, regardless of which region of the world they came from.

But there was more. Lilly remembered the strange feeling she had when she faced them. In some inexplicable way, a new kind of awareness emerged in her. On the way back to Utah, she had felt the urge to talk to Walker about it, comparing that moment to a colorblind person suddenly being able to see colors or a child recognizing herself in the mirror for the first time.

The Neanderthals had their own charisma. As a life form, they were unique, not just in terms of their immense skulls. The oracular glow from the depths of their eye sockets, their ability to magically make themselves invisible in the most obvious situations, their immeasurable connection with nature—all this was quite extraordinary. Lilly had to reorganize her worldview.

"Is that you, Spirit?"

She recognized the approaching timber wolf with its piercing yellow eyes right away. She crouched down, hugged it joyfully, and scratched its chest fur affectionately. The predator made itself small in front of her and licked her chin incessantly. How strange and beautiful it was to see Spirit on the loose! It was the first time she had seen him in the wild, the habitat he was supposed to have.

There were probably other runaways roaming the grounds, overjoyed to have escaped the enclosure. This was an absolute disaster for her wolf park as an institution. Strictly speaking, Lilly would have to inform the authorities immediately and pull out all the stops to get the matter under control. Far more important than the regulations of the state nature conservation authority, however, was the group of Neanderthals who had been hiding from humanity in their secret paradise since time immemorial, restricting their freedom to survive. Omu could not be allowed to fall into the hands of the authorities. He had to return to the protection of the sinkhole as quickly as possible, back to Kela and her people.

At that moment, Walker wished he could make himself invisible, too. With the two of them firmly in sight, he entrenched himself between the helicopter skids under the fuselage of the Hummingbird and hardly dared to breathe. The thought of being tracked down and attacked by a colossal male wolf at any moment was highly unsettling. At least he held the loaded tranquillizer gun in his hands while the two companions greeted each other exuberantly.

His head was also full of memories of the wondrous Stone Age journey, which, as a scientist, he could not have imagined in greater detail. Even the Holy Grail of personal encounters with early humans in the flesh, which none of his colleagues had even dared to dream of, was granted to him. Countless gaps in the Neanderthal puzzle had been filled.

However, a largely completed picture of this wondrous human form did not make them any less puzzling. Rudimentary and wise at the same time, they had found a way to be sedentary without causing even the slightest damage to their habitat, and one had to seriously wonder which way of life was the wiser: theirs or that of our so-called civilization.

Publicizing the events of the past few days could probably make them both—Lilly and him—rich and famous. As explorers, they would be immortal. However, revealing the jewel of the primeval valley was out of the question. No, they would forever keep to themselves the existence of what was, in all probability, the last population of Neanderthals that hardly anyone would ever venture to believe.

Spirit suddenly let go of his caretaker and looked back at the direction from which he had come. There he stood: Omu, battered and tired, though solid as a rock. Omu, a fine specimen of a Neanderthal, scowled at Lilly and looked through her at the helicopter behind her. Omu: the relentless hunter, dressed in Stone Age clothing, extremely muscular, covered with plant parts in all shades of earth, ear and shoulder smeared with blood and loess and growling like a bear between attack and defense.

For what felt like an eternity, Lilly was paralyzed by him. The oppressive tension of the moment was only relieved by Spirit, who trotted carefree toward the Neanderthal with a soft "woof". Omu ignored the wolf until he was close to him, and then he let out a short, commanding sound with which he instantly subdued him. Spirit turned onto his back without resistance and lay still.

Only now did Lilly manage to relax and slowly straighten up. The Neanderthal did not take his eyes off her. Omu recognized Watka's shiny horn hanging around the blonde woman's shoulder and moved closer to her, step by step, until he was only a body length away from her. *Give me what belongs to my people!*

Lilly forced herself to smile as she gently removed the buffalo horn and humbly held it out to him. But the horn was not what Omu craved. Not joy, but mistrust and pain were written all over his face. In vain, he searched her entirely for the spearhead. Lilly had never seen such an expression of disappointment in her life.

"I don't have it," she whispered, shaking her head and fervently hoping that he would understand the meaning of her words. "It's with your people." Lilly pointed north. "We know where your clan is hiding. It's far, but we know the place."

The early man tilted his head, straining to understand what the bobo woman was saying:

Lilly continued: "Watka, Kela, Hani—they're there too."

Omu's ears twitched and he moved even closer to her. Had he heard the names of his companions?

"Watka, Kela, Hani," he repeated in a warm, sonorous voice and a hint of hope flitted across his face.

"Yes, and you are Omu." She pointed at him, and then out into the vast expanse of the forest. "Your family is waiting for you. We can take you to them."

Spirit leapt to his paws in a single bound. Akecheta had stepped out of the side bushes into the clearing and aimed his modern hunting bow directly at the Neanderthal. Omu had been oblivious to his surroundings for minutes and now could not take cover in time. One false move and the hunting arrow would accelerate in his direction in just twenty milliseconds.

However, Omu did not face the archer alone. With only one arrow on the string, Akecheta was forced to choose a target: the early man or the snarling wolf at his side, ready to strike.

Hesitantly, he pointed the arrow alternately at Omu and then back at the timber wolf. The powerful wolf raised his hackles but remained waiting at the side of the early man, who seemed to be mentally in control of his will.

Akecheta kept his longbow fully drawn, which he could not keep up for long. After a short time, the draw weight began to sap his strength, and he became increasingly breathless from the exertion. Shooting the arrow would give him immediate relief but, at the same time, make him vulnerable.

"Don't do it!" Lilly implored him. "He's not dangerous. Trust me!"

The Indian was unsettled and hesitated, and both his strength and conviction were fading rapidly. He began to tremble violently, his neck tensed up, and the pressure in the muscles between his shoulder blades and spine became unbearable.

"Please, don't do it!"

He held out for a few more seconds, and then, with a sound of exhaustion, he relaxed his hunting bow, dropped it and the arrow to the ground, and bowed his head. He gave up.

Courageously, Lilly walked up to him, put her hand on his shoulder and said: "Thank you, my friend."

At that moment, a shot rang out under the Hummingbird. High-pressure carbon dioxide propelled the feathered projectile through the barrel of the stun gun and forty feet through the air into Omu's thick thigh. Walker had aimed well. The plunger of the tranquillizer dart injected five milligrams of modified Hellabrunn mixture into the muscle tissue.

Shocked, Omu pulled out the empty syringe and wheeled around angrily in search of the shooter. *What happened? Where did this come from?* When the anesthetic kicked in, he panicked, snatched the buffalo horn from Lilly's hand and ran down the slope, staggering until he tripped and fell into the grass.

Spirit, Lilly, and Akecheta ran straight to him. He had lost consciousness. Now, time was of the essence.

"Help me!" Lilly begged the Shadow Wolf. "Into the helicopter with him!"

Together, they dragged the leaden Neanderthal to the rescue aircraft. Walker was already on board and pulled him in with all his might.

"Please, don't tell on us," Lilly called out to Akecheta after she had also got in. "He's not a monster; he's a Native American. Just like your ancestors."

Walker took a seat in the cockpit. The tank was well filled, and the medical equipment was working perfectly. While the Australian started up the machine, Lilly strapped the sedated passenger onto a stretcher and connected him to the diagnostic equipment, which was linked to a multifunction monitor. This allowed her to monitor all vital signs during the flight: heart rate, blood pressure, oxygen saturation, temperature and breathing gas. She would maintain the anesthesia until landing.

Akecheta waved thoughtfully behind them as they climbed up from the clearing of the Deer Hill.

Spirit was already back in the woods.

53

The grotto at the entrance to the primeval valley has become Kela's territory. Here, she rests, works, and watches day and night. No one will dispute her place because no one believes in Omu's return more than she does. Every day of waiting gnaws at her, but she is tenacious and unwavering.

"If you two stay connected, everything will fall into place," Watka reassured her. "As distant as your mortal shells are, nothing can separate you forever."

Today, however, everything is different: Kela can't feel him. For the first time, he feels truly distant. Inside herself, she searches for her beloved but finds nothing except emptiness. She calls out to him, but he remains silent, as if he has fallen into a raging river, as if rushing whirlpools and foaming masses of water are dragging him to the bottom of the lake, as if he has fallen into a deep and lasting sleep.

Where are you?

Feeling emptier and more deserted than ever before, she crawls into the darkest corner of the rocky cave. There, she hopes to catch a tiny spark of him. She repeats Watka's words over and over again:

"If you stay connected, everything will fall into place."

But what can she believe in when nothing but darkness envelops her, and the soft roaring of the waterfall is the only thing she can hear?

Suddenly, there is another sound. Almost imperceptible at first, then louder and louder, the gentle murmur of the countless drops is joined by rapid, individual strokes so rhythmic and decisive that they soon completely drown out the constant, faint roar of the waterfall.

Full of fear, Kela presses herself even deeper into the protective niche. Is this the end or the beginning? She would almost prefer either one.

Soon, the pounding is so fierce that it sounds as if a wild herd of buffalo is trampling everything down to the mountain lake. Kela covers her ears, whimpering. The storm of roaring animals whips the spray into the cave. The noise penetrates ever more loudly and violently.

The roaring hurricane continues for a while. Finally, the pounding rises again and disappears into the vastness of the sky. The storm subsides. It is over.

The young Neanderthal woman gets up, trembling and weak. Brothers and sisters call out to her, climbing toward her, one by one, from the primeval valley through the stone arch. A hunter hesitantly penetrates the falling water and glides into the bright outside world. Others follow him.

Then, Kela also steps out into the glistening light. Because she has been in the darkness for so long, she can barely open her eyes, but she can hear well.

"Omu-gat-wanna!" the crowd shouts to her from the shore of the lake. "Omu is back!"

It is not the end, but a new beginning, and the proud, sustaining sound of the buffalo horn announces it to their world.

Afterword

One of my ancestors was a doctor, another an archaeologist and another a Neanderthal. There is a part of all of them in me. Perhaps that is why this book came into being.

Neanderthals, Beringian Wolves, Salish, Luzon People, Shadow Wolves, and almost all creatures and places mentioned in the novel actually existed or still exist today. The Feron Wolf Park is fictional.

I would like to thank my sister Natalie for her initial suggestions, and Bruce Todhunter, Patrick Keeney, and Luke Reeves for editing the English version of the book.

Thanks also to Nobel Prize winner Svante Pääbo, who answered some of my questions in writing.

The book is dedicated to my mother.

More information:

https://intotheshadowland.webflow.io/

www.ingramcontent.com/pod-product-compliance
Lightning Source LLC
Chambersburg PA
CBHW070102260626
47160CB00004B/1290